Harold stared at Fred in astonishment.

"Are you suggesting," he said in his most pompous tone "that Madge here would for one moment consider someone like you?"

"I am," said Fred.

He nodded to Madge.

"Ask her. Let Madge make the choice."

"I will indeed," said Harold.

He put back his glasses, and turned to Madge.

"Are you coming back to dance with me, or staying here with this nasty piece of work?"

Harold waited, supremely confident.

They both looked at Madge.

It seemed like an eternity, but it was probably five or ten seconds. Madge knew this was the most important decision she would probably make in her life. And she also knew which way she wanted to go.

She went to Fred's side, and put her hand in his.

"I'm staying," she said.

Harold stared at her, in hurt and disbelief. Fred smiled and led Madge back to the car.

And with those words, Madge sealed her fate forever.

Neighbours™

THE RAMSAYS
A FAMILY DIVIDED!

Written by
VALDA MARSHALL
& RAY KOLLE

Based on the **Grundy Television Series**
as shown on BBC Television

Mandarin

A Mandarin Paperback

NEIGHBOURS

First published in Great Britain 1989
by Mandarin Paperbacks
Michelin House, 81 Fulham Road, London SW3 6RB

Mandarin is an imprint of the Octopus Publishing Group

Neighbours™ & © 1989 Grundy Television Pty Limited

A CIP catalogue record for this book is available from
the British Library.

ISBN 0 7493 0055 8

Printed in Great Britain by Cox & Wyman, Reading

Chapter 1

BRISBANE, Queensland. 1965.
It was one of those humid, steamy nights when everything seemed to slow down and stop. Through the open windows of the local Arts Institute, where the dance was being held, the scent of frangipanni and hibiscus mixed with the smell of cigarettes from dancers who'd gone out for a smoke. The four-piece band was taking a supper break.

Madge knew she'd worn the wrong dress, but it was too late now. Her mother, Edna, had urged her to wear the white cotton — the one she'd made for her last birthday. But Madge had never liked it. It was the kind of dress that mothers tend to make for their daughters . . . demure, sedate, with little puffed sleeves. Instead, Madge had put on the blue nylon that showed off her figure to advantage. But right now it was clinging to her in damp, uncomfortable sticky patches of perspiration.

1

As Madge tried to cool off, fanning herself with a program, she could see Harold battling with the crowds at the supper table. Dear Harold. He was trying to be polite, and not get in anyone's way. At the same time, he was determined to get his rightful share of sandwiches and orange drink (the entrance tickets had specified "Light Refreshments Incl.")

Harold caught Madge's eye, and gave her a signal. The signal said he was trying, just be patient. Madge sighed, and fanned herself again. It sometimes seemed to her that half her time with Harold was spent being patient. He was not a pushy person, that was his trouble. Reliable, yes. And hardworking. One day he'd take over his father's stock and station agency. Meantime, he was learning the business and taking Madge out in whatever free time he had.

Harold gave Madge another signal that said he was making headway, and then he disappeared into the crowd. She forgot him for the moment, and looked around the hall to see what else was happening.

Over in a far corner she could see Lou Carpenter chatting up a striking-looking redhead in a lowcut dress. Lou caught her eye and waved, then turned back to the redhead.

They were very close, heads together, talking in low tones. Then she saw them leave the hall, and guessed where they were going . . . to some secluded spot to neck, in Lou's new red sportscar.

Madge watched them with the same kind of feelings she used to have when she was a small girl, her nose pressed against the window of an expensive toy-shop — envious, admiring, but realistic enough to know she had no hope of getting any of the things inside.

Lou was like that . . . unattainable. She had pined after him when they were at High School together, and he had been the good-looking, popular captain of the football team. He had scarcely been aware of her, preferring the more flashy types. She wasn't his kind of girl.

Whose kind of girl was she?

Harold's, according to her parents, Dan and Edna Ramsay. They approved of Harold. She knew it, by the way they kept asking her to invite him home for Sunday roast. Harold also thought she was his kind of girl. She could tell by the way he looked at her, the way he held her hand tightly when they sat in the back row stalls at the movies. He always behaved like a perfect gentleman, never venturing more than a chaste kiss. Once, when he had accidentally touched her breast during an embrace in the front seat of his car, he had been acutely embarrassed and apologised. It was all Madge could do to stop

3

herself from smiling.

Madge was very fond of Harold, and she supposed that some day they would probably get
married. He had hinted a couple of times he was
saving towards their future.

"Hi, Madge . . . how's it going, kiddo?"

It was Max, her older brother, with an attractive dark-haired girl she recognised as Maria
Rossie, daughter of one of his workmates. Max
was working as a plumber on a building site, and
had told her about Franco Rossie, the Italian
tiler he was helping to speak English. It was a bit
of a family joke. Tom, her other brother, reckoned the only words Max had taught Franco so
far were "flamin' cow" and "my bloody oath."
But they were good mates, and Max seemed
keen on the daughter.

There was someone else with Max and Maria,
a tall, blonde young man who seemed to be on
his own. Max introduced him as Fred Mitchell,
and said they'd met at the pub.

"He's just lobbed in town," said Max. "I told
him this is where you meet all the good sorts."

Fred grinned at Madge, a crooked smile that
said: I'm a bit of a rogue, but a nice bloke really.
Madge understood, and smiled back. It was like
a shared joke.

The musicians, fortified by nips of rum and
whiskey in their soft drinks out the back of the

hall, came back and took their places once again. The emcee went to the microphone.

"Take your partners for the next dance," he announced.

Max looked around the hall.

"Where's Harold?"

Madge gestured towards the supper table, where she could still see Harold anxiously bobbing around, his spectacles glinting under the lights. He had a plate of sandwiches now in one hand, but was still queuing for the drinks.

Fred Mitchell looked over as well, and then back at Madge.

"In that case, may I have this dance?" he asked.

Madge hesitated a fraction, and glanced again at Harold — who now appeared to be having a violent argument with a large, fat man in the queue ahead of him.

"Go on, Madge," urged Max. "Be a sport."

As Madge went into Fred's arms, something strange happened. She felt a tingle, which started at the nape of her neck and worked its way right down her spine. It was like static electricity, something she had never experienced before.

With Harold's arms around her, she felt warm and protected. But with this stranger, it was different. For one thing, he held her closer than

5

Harold ever did. So close, she felt breathless. Or was it just the way he was looking at her, as they went around the floor.

"How old are you, Madge Ramsay?" he was asking.

Madge told him. Nineteen.

"Just right," said Fred. And there was that crooked grin again.

Right for what? Madge wondered.

Just at that moment they whirled past Harold, who didn't see them and was walking back. He'd won his battle with the fat man, and was carrying the sandwiches and two glasses of orange juice.

Harold reached the table, looked around for Madge without finding her, and sat down.

"I should get back," said Madge.

Fred looked at her.

"D'you want to?"

Madge suddenly threw all caution to the winds.

"No," she said.

Fred pulled her even more tightly to him, until she could hardly breathe. Then he looked down at her, a twinkle in his eyes.

"Tell me all about yourself," he said.

And Madge told him. She told him about her parents, Edna and Dan, and how they'd battled to bring up their three children, Madge, Max and

Tom. She told him about Erinsborough down south, where she'd grown up as a child. A street in Erinsborough, Ramsay Street, had been named after her grandfather Jack, who had been one of the pioneers in the district and had twice been Mayor.

Madge was enormously proud of her grandfather, and had happy memories of the time she lived in the area. Dan and Edna used to point out the place to her where Jack had built his original homestead on an orchard, and tell her that one day the land would belong to Madge and her two brothers.

Madge could vaguely remember Grandfather Jack, who used to always carry strong white peppermints in his pocket . . . and had a large beard that prickled when he kissed her.

There were family picnics in the old orchard, long since rundown and full of weeds. Every week, as the land was sub-divided, new houses would spring up and new people move in.

Then Dan lost his job, and decided he could do better for his family if he moved north. They went to Brisbane, and bought a modest timber house in an outer suburb.

Jack Ramsay died. Madge could still remember the day the news came, and her feeling of sadness. Of all the grandchildren, she had been the one closest to him.

"Have you ever been back to Ramsay Street?" asked Fred.

Madge shook her head. There was nothing to go back to . . . just some friends from early days at school, but she'd lost touch with most of them. One, Jim Robinson, occasionally wrote to Max.

She'd put Ramsay Street behind her, as had her parents. They'd now made a new life for themselves in Queensland.

"That's enough about me," said Madge. "Tell me about yourself."

He told her he was a sales representative, dealing in a new line of plumber's hardware. That's how he struck up the acquaintance with Max in the pub — Max had noticed him open his briefcase, and go through some advertising material.

They were now back at the table, and Harold had seen them.

He stood up stiffly, as Fred steered Madge by her elbow back to her seat.

Madge introduced them, and Harold put his hand out.

"A pleasure," he said. "Any friend of Madge is a friend of mine."

For the first time, Madge thought how pompous and stuffy Harold sounded. She glanced at Fred, to see his reaction. Fred just grinned, and thanked Madge for the dance. When he walked away, Madge felt a sense of loss.

She was still thinking about Fred, and wondering if Harold would be angry because she'd danced with him when she realised Harold was talking to her.

"You'd think they'd organise the catering a bit better," he was saying. "Fancy running out of orange cordial. I had to stand and wait until they made some more."

It was so Harold that Madge almost laughed out loud.

She started eating a sandwich, but her eyes kept searching for Fred.

Tom wandered over to talk to them. He was with Doreen Leicester, one of the nurses from the local hospital. Madge liked Doreen. She wasn't a raving beauty, but she had a soft, natural charm that made people instantly warm to her. Madge always felt if she had a problem, Doreen would be the kind of person she'd go to talk to.

And she had brains, too. She'd topped her last year in the nursing exams. But Madge had a feeling Doreen wouldn't be a nurse for much longer. Tom had confided to her that they already had an "understanding," and when they married he wanted to start a family as soon as possible.

9

"How's tricks, Harold?" asked Tom, giving Harold a slap on the back that almost dislodged his spectacles. That was Tom, always the joker. Harold adjusted them, and tried to look his most dignified.

"Fine . . . fine, Tom," he answered. "And how is everything with you?"

"Couldn't be better, matey," said Tom, giving Doreen an affectionate squeeze.

"Mind you, I've got a great little sheila here to keep me in line. The ladies . . . what would we do without them?"

"What, indeed," agreed Harold, looking at Madge and taking her hand. Any other time Madge would have enjoyed Harold's display of affection. Now, for some reason, she just felt uncomfortable.

Tom and Doreen left, and Harold asked Madge for the next dance. As they got up to take to the dance floor, Harold reached in a pocket, took out a pair of white cotton gloves, and put them on.

"D'you have to wear those things, Harold?" asked Madge.

Again, she felt vaguely irritated without knowing why. Wearing white gloves to a dance had long been a habit of Harold's, even though Madge had once pointed out to him that he was the only man in his age group to do it.

10

Harold looked hurt.

"I'm only trying to protect your dress, Madge," he said. "It's just common courtesy and good manners."

Madge sighed, as she dropped the subject and they danced around the floor. She liked Harold, but why did he always have to sound as though he was born middleaged?

*   *   *

The dance finished with a spatter of applause, and the emcee took the microphone again. The lights suddenly dimmed, and then began twirling . . . spraying a myriad of coloured patterns on the ceiling.

"All right, gentlemen . . . here's your chance to meet the lady of your dreams. Take your partners for the Excuse Me Waltz."

Harold looked down at Madge."

"Shall we sit this one out?" he asked.

Normally Madge would have said yes. She knew what it would be like . . . a succession of men who'd come to the dance on their own with the idea of picking up a girl to take home — preferably with the promise of more than a kiss at the end of it. She hated the way they pawed her, or held her so close she could smell their

11

beer-sodden breath in her face. These were the desperates, loners on a single ticket, hoping their five shillings would buy them a cheap thrill. Normally men on their own weren't allowed in . . . it was supposed to be couples only. But somehow they got through.

This time some sixth sense made Madge decide to keep dancing. And she knew she'd done the right thing when after two or more rounds of the floor, Fred Mitchell tapped Harold on the shoulder.

"Excuse me," he said, and there was that lopsided grin again.

Harold had to stand aside, as Fred took Madge in his arms. Madge left him standing forlornly on the floor as Fred whirled her away.

Suddenly they were outside the hall, and in the semi-tropical darkness. The air was still and close, with an inky blue sky above. The only stars in sight were the Southern Cross.

"Where are we going?" asked Madge, as Fred led her away from the hall.

"You'll see," he said.

She saw. Fred headed for a car parked under a tree, and motioned her to get in.

Madge couldn't believe what she was doing. Although she was as adventurous as the rest of the girls in her crowd, years of strict upbringing by Edna had left their mark. Boys don't marry a girl who comes too easy . . . don't kiss on a first date, he won't respect you . . . don't get into cars with strangers . . . don't . . . don't . . . don't . . .

Madge climbed into the car.

It was though she were two people. One kept firing warning signals, urging her to be cautious. The other was saying that this was the most interesting and attractive man she'd ever met.

Fred didn't attempt to neck, or even kiss her. (One to me, Mum, Madge made a mental note.) Instead, he began asking her more about herself, and Madge found herself talking as naturally and easily as if she'd known him for years.

She told him how she'd done a business course, and was now working in an office. She told him of her plans to one day move out from home, and share a flat with a girlfriend. She'd already saved 125 pounds towards it. Not that she didn't love her parents . . . but because she wanted to try a little independence.

And Fred also talked about himself. He told how he'd come from a family of battlers, with his father eking out a living in the late thirties from selling clothes props door to door. Most of the time he was unemployed and on the dole. When war came, he'd joined up and got the first regular pay in his life. His dad had thought things would be better when the war finished, and he came home again. But they were worse. Nobody wanted clothes props any more. So he turned to drink, while Fred's mother went out and scrubbed office floors. They wanted washing machines.

"The Government should have helped him," said Madge, indignant. "After all, he was a soldier."

"You don't know my old man," said Fred. "He's a no-hoper . . . always will be. I tell you Madge, I'm never going to wind up like that . . . scrounging around, asking people for handouts. I want to run my own life. No one's going to tell Fred Mitchell what to do."

Madge noticed that his arm was now around her shoulder, but she didn't mind. All right, Edna, so you won . . .

Fred looked down at her.

"Y'know, Madge Ramsay, you're a very pretty girl."

The tingle began to climb her spine again.

*   *   *

Back at the dance, Harold was looking around the hall . . . puzzled.

He went over to Tom and Doreen.

"Have you seen Madge anywhere?" he asked.

14

Tom nodded towards the open side door.

"I saw her going out with that new bloke," he said. "Maybe they're getting a bit of fresh air."

Harold frowned. He didn't particularly like that Fred Mitchell when he met him, and he liked him even less now. He'd warned Madge time after time against getting mixed up with riff-raff. And this stranger felt like trouble. He was too cocky and self-assured by far, the kind who would latch on to a girl and make a nuisance of himself.

Harold knew exactly what had happened. The man had taken advantage of Madge's good nature, and was boring her silly with talk about himself. And Madge was too kind and polite to give him the brush-off. She was probably out there, listening, and bored stiff.

Well, he'd rescue her from it.

Harold strode purposefully from the hall, and glanced around. There were several couples in twos and groups, talking and having a smoke. But no sign of Madge and Fred. He began to walk towards the car park.

In the car, Fred had stopped talking. He still had his arm around Madge, but it was a tighter grip now. He pulled her closer, so her head was almost on his shoulder.

Madge felt excitement stirring.

She began to say something, anything, to keep

things on a casual basis . . . when Fred suddenly pulled her to him and kissed her. It wasn't like one of Harold's prim closed-lips kisses — this one fired her with wild emotions she'd never known before. The tingle exploded into fireworks.

They were still kissing when Harold found them.

He pulled open the driver's door, and angrily hauled Fred out.

"You unmitigated swine," said Harold.

Then he took off his spectacles, and threw a punch. It was a wild one, and only grazed Fred's chin. But it was enough for Fred to angrily retaliate.

The next minute, a shocked Madge saw the two of them hitting each other in a wild fight. Harold was the heavier of the two, but Fred had skill and speed. In a moment or two, Madge saw blood trickling down from Harold's nose on to his immaculate white shirt.

"Stop it!" cried Madge. "Please, both of you . . . stop it this instant!!"

Neither took any notice, but kept wildly punching.

Then Harold grabbed Fred, caught him off balance, and the two of them were rolling around on the ground. The white gloves fell from Harold's pocket, and lay in the dirt unnoticed.

16

Madge was almost in tears.

By this time a small group of people had heard the commotion, and were standing around. One was Lou Carter, without the redhead.

"Good on you, Harold," said Lou. "Hit the bloody bastard."

Fred got to his feet again, and the two men paused to take breath. Harold glared at Fred, his anger showing by the way his bottom lip was quivering.

"You . . . you . . . slimey rough-neck . . . Why don't you find your own girl, and leave mine alone?"

Fred glared back.

"Why don't you ask Madge what she wants?" he said. "Ask her which one of us she prefers."

Harold stared at Fred in astonishment.

"Are you suggesting," he said in his most pompous tone "that Madge here would for one moment consider someone like you?"

"I am," said Fred.

He nodded to Madge.

"Ask her. Let Madge make the choice."

"I will indeed," said Harold.

He put back his glasses, and turned to Madge.

"Are you coming back to dance with me, or staying here with this nasty piece of work?"

Harold waited, supremely confident.

They both looked at Madge.

17

It seemed like an eternity, but it was probably five or ten seconds. Madge knew this was the most important decision she would probably make in her life. And she also knew which way she wanted to go.

She went to Fred's side, and put her hand in his.

"I'm staying," she said.

Harold stared at her, in hurt and disbelief. Fred smiled and led Madge back to the car.

And with those words, Madge sealed her fate forever.

*   *   *

Chapter 2

COFFS Harbour, northern New South Wales. 1985.

Madge stormed into the living room, a pile of papers in her hand. Fred, sitting in his favourite armchair watching the races on the telly, a beer on the table alongside him, barely looked up. But Charlene, 15, and Henry, 17, exchanged worried glances. Mum was on the warpath again.

"Look at these," said Madge, waving the papers in front of Fred's face.

"Bills, all of them. Some go back three months."

"So what?" said Fred, concentrating on the television.

Madge was almost at the screaming point.

"So they should have been paid ages ago. I thought we were doing all right, and now I find these . . . at the back of a drawer in our bedroom. Why didn't you tell me about them, instead of shoving them out of sight?''

Fred frowned, and tried to hear what the T.V. commentator was saying. But Madge's shouting drowned out the announcement of who won the third race.

''Gorblimey, can't you give a man a bit of peace on a Saturday afternoon?'' he asked. ''I had ten bucks on that photo finish, and now I don't know which one has won.''

Madge walked over to the set, and quite deliberately turned it off.

''I still want to know why these were at the back of your drawer?'' she demanded.

Fred sighed. He knew he'd get no peace from Madge unless he gave her some kind of answer.

Susan gave them to me, and asked me what I wanted her to do with them. I put them on one side, and just forgot. That's all . . . it's not the end of the world. Now will you bloody well turn that telly on again, and let me find out whether I've won anything?''

''Turn it on yourself,'' snapped Madge.

Charlene leaped up, and pressed the switch on the set for her father.

''Thanks, Princess,'' said Fred, smiling at her.

Charlene smiled back. She loved her father, and hated it when Madge put on one of her screaming tantrums.

Madge's face tightened, and she went back to

their bedroom where she was doing a springclean. As she put the bills to one side, and turned on the vacuum cleaner, she decided to have a word with Susan first thing Monday morning.

Susan Cole was the young girl hired to help run the office in the hardware shop Madge and Fred owned in Coffs Harbour. They had bought in cheaply, because the previous owner had let it run down to a point where it was losing money. Fred hadn't been keen at first, but Madge had talked him into it — pointing out that with her business training, she could run the office side of it . . . leaving Fred to concentrate on selling. And that was something Fred was definitely good at. He had a cheeky charm and persuasive manner that Madge always said could sell refrigerators to Eskimos — look at the way he'd talked her into marrying him, within six months of them meeting. And he'd done an even more impressive con job on her father, Dan, who had almost thrown Fred out of the house when he found out Madge preferred him to Harold.

At first Dan had refused to give permission for them to marry. But Madge turned 20, and pointed out she only had another year to go before she could do exactly what she liked. And Dan found it hard to say "no" to his only daughter. It was finally Edna, realising that Madge was head over heels in love, who finally persuaded Dan to sign the papers and give Madge a proper wedding. But she knew how much Dan hated walking down the aisle with her, knowing that it was Fred — and not Harold — waiting at the altar the other end.

Having given permission, Dan had grudgingly done what he could. He had given them money as a wedding present, and offered to help them find a place to live in Brisbane. But there had been so much bitterness and animosity, that Madge decided it would be better to start their married life away from her parents.

Coffs Harbour, in the heart of banana-growing country on the north coast of New South Wales, had always appealed to her when they had gone there on holidays. And it was close enough so she could slip up to Brisbane to see her family any time she wanted. Fred, fortunately, had agreed.

So here they were, living in a weatherboard house in a street lined with palms and flame trees, and making a reasonable living. If only Fred would concentrate more on the business, and less on horses and women . . .

Madge frowned, as she thought of the last episode — a customer, Leonie Sampson, whose husband spent a lot of time away on business.

Fred had made a point of delivering any orders himself, and staying away from the shop as long as two hours at a time. Madge had had her suspicions, but hadn't done anything about it. Until the afternoon when Fred was away nearly three hours, and she asked Susan to mind the shop while she went out. Madge went to Leonie's house, and saw Fred's car parked in the garage. The back door was unlocked, and she walked in. Fred and Leonie were in bed together.

Madge had threatened that time to leave Fred, and she meant it. But Fred, knowing he couldn't run the business without Madge, had talked his way out of it as usual. He promised it would never happen again. It was the last time he'd ever look at another woman, said Fred. But the memory of it still hurt.

Back in the living room, Fred finished his beer and looked at Charlene.

"Like to do a good turn for your old dad?" he asked. The crooked smile and the charm worked on Charlene the same as it had for her mother twenty years ago. She jumped up, went to the kitchen, and brought him back another cold beer. He gave her an affectionate squeeze as she gave him the can. Fred knew his daughter adored him, and he worked on it. Henry, on the other hand, was a different matter. Fred had never had much time for Henry, who had been a precocious child . . . and in and out of trouble almost as soon as he hit his teenage years. And part of Fred's dislike was because he knew Henry was the apple of Madge's eye. Fred considered Madge was too soft on the boy, and told her so. Madge put Henry's scrapes down to high spirits.

When Henry announced at fifteen he was leaving school, Madge was upset. But Fred's view was to let him go. At least he wouldn't be footing school bills for him all the time, not to mention pocket-money so Henry could take out his girls.

If he wants to take out birds, let him pay for it himself — that was Fred's attitude. And Madge, who often slipped Henry the odd five dollars behind Fred's back, was forced for once to agree. Maybe Henry would be better taking a job and earning some money. It might give him a sense of responsibility. But it didn't work out that way. Henry's jobs were few and far between, and he didn't hold them for long. In between, he went on the dole. Henry's hobby, and he worked hard at it, was having fun.

Madge finished the vacuuming, switched off the power, and then took out a duster to clean down the woodwork. She loved the house, and took pride in it.

Madge remembered the day she and Fred decided to buy it. They'd been living in a caravan park near the ocean when they first arrived in Coffs Harbour back in 1965. It was cheap and convenient, and it gave them a chance to look around and decide what to do.

Fred had given up his job as a sales representative, and was thinking of going into used cars. But Madge had spotted this advertisement in The Advocate, asking for someone to buy a hardware shop. The price was a bargain, just the cost of stock and fittings. The business was so rundown that the owner didn't even ask for goodwill. She and Fred went to have a look, and Madge saw the possibilities right away. It was one of those shops that sold everything . . . hardware, paint, pots and pans, garden fertiliser. The place was covered in dust, and some of the stock had been lying there for years. But Coffs Harbour was a small place just beginning to boom, and a lot of people were moving there from the south to escape the cold winters. Madge could see the possibilities.

They bought the business, staying in the caravan park for the first year. Madge rolled up her sleeves, and cleaned the place, scrubbing it from top to bottom. Then she got credit for Fred to buy new stock, and kept the books while Fred drummed up business. The local people liked Fred, he was a good mixer always good for a beer and a yarn. Business began to take off, and at the end of the first year they were making a small profit.

At the end of year two, Fred and Madge had made enough to consider a down payment on a small home . . . a three-bedroom timber house, with a view from the front window of the hills studded with banana palms on the slopes. Next year, Madge found herself pregnant.

Henry came into the room as Madge was wiping down the window-sill.

"Can you lend me a few bucks?" he asked.

Madge put down the duster, and looked at Henry in exasperation.

"What d'you mean, lend . . .?" she asked. "I haven't seen the last lot I gave you. What's it for this time?"

Henry came up to her, put his arms around Madge's waist, and nuzzled her neck.

"It's just that I've promised this girl I'd meet her at the milkbar. And I'm broke until my next dole cheque comes through. Then I'll pay back, honest."

He ruffled her hair, and gave her the first force of his dazzling smile. Despite herself, Madge couldn't help a sudden gust of affection for this her firstborn. He'd been a beautiful baby, all blonde curls and blue eyes. And he'd grown into a handsome young man, with the same winning charm as his father. Trouble was, he knew it.

Madge went to her handbag, took out five dollars, and gave it to him.

"Just make sure it's a girl you're spending it on, and not some of your no good mates," she said. "I saw Jacko the other day, and he was prowling around High Street looking into cars. You keep mixing with him and you're heading for trouble."

"Jacko's okay," said Henry, pocketing the five dollars before Madge could change her mind. "He just likes anything on wheels."

"Preferably other people's," said Madge, but Henry was relieved to see she was now smiling. She could never stay mad at Henry for long.

"What's Charlene doing?" asked Madge, as she put her handbag back in the wardrobe. "Is she going with you?"

"Search me." said Henry, shrugging. "Why don't you ask Lennie yourself?"

That name "Lennie" — Madge winced as she heard it. Why did Henry and all Charlene's friends have to call her that?

Madge couldn't ask Charlene anything these days, but she didn't tell Henry. Instead, she shoo-ed him out, so she could get on with the cleaning. Madge sighed, as Henry left. If only

Charlene were as easy to get along with. But Charlene always seemed to have a chip on her shoulder, at least where Madge was concerned. Nothing Madge said or did ever got through to her. And she resented anything Madge told her to do, things like making her bed in the mornings before she left for school. Charlene wanted to leave at fifteen, as Henry had done. But Madge refused to allow it, and this time Fred was on her side. So Charlene was full of simmering resentment, which she took out in defiance or outright rudeness. Who said girls were easier to raise than boys?

Madge finished the dusting, and then decided to sort the dirty laundry and put a couple of loads through the machine. Once she got into a cleaning mood, it was hard to stop.

She stripped the sheets from the bed, and checked through her personal things. Then she went to the wardrobe, and looked through the clothes Fred had hanging there. The trouble with Fred was that he put his dirty shirts back in the wardrobe, instead of in the laundry basket. She was always at him about it, but he still kept doing it.

Madge did her usual check through pockets, just in case something had been left in them. It was then that she discovered the letter.

The shock was almost as great as the time

28

Madge had walked in on Fred and Leonie. The letter was from a woman, and it was obvious from the tone of it that she and Fred were having an affair. Only this time it wasn't Leonie. It was some name Madge had never heard of before.

Madge stood with the letter in her hand, trembling. Then she walked into the living room, where Henry and Charlene were packing up the Scrabble set, and confronted Fred.

"What's the meaning of this?" she asked.

At first Fred thought it was just another bill, and prepared to ignore it. Then he recognised the writing, and knew he'd been caught out. He immediately decided the best tactic was to go on the offensive.

"You've got a nerve, going through my personal things," he said. "Give me that!"

Madge hung on to the letter, waving it in the air, as Charlene and Henry escaped through the front door. They weren't sure what it was all about, but they had been through this kind of thing enough times to know it was leading up to yet another blazing row.

Fred grabbed for the letter. Madge grimly hung on to it.

"You're not getting it back until you explain yourself," said Madge. "I'm sick and tired of working my fingers to the bone, trying to keep the business going, while you waste your time chasing after every woman who gives you a second look. If you paid more attention to the shop, and less to every floosy who gives you the come-on, we'd both be better off.''

Fred decided to change tactics.

"Why'd you think I look at other women in the first place?'' he demanded. ''Because I'm not getting any comfort at home, that's why. A man's only human. All you seem to do these days is nag, nag, nag. If you spent a bit more time in doing what any decent wife should do, and that's looking after your husband, then I wouldn't go wandering in the first place. A fridge has got more warmth than you have. Why don't you wake up to yourself for a change?''

Madge stood there, the letter still in her hand, livid with rage and hurt. Fred's shot had found its mark.

"You rotten bastard,'' she suddenly screamed. ''You filthy, rotten, lying cheat! I work my guts out for you, and this is all the thanks I get . . .''

Fred decided he'd had enough. Madge at her best wasn't always easy to get along with. But when she was in a vile temper, as she was now, retreat was the best policy.

He put on his jacket, and stormed from the house.

Left on her own, Madge suddenly wondered where it was all going to end. She sat down in a chair, letting the letter fall to the ground. The woman, whoever she was, didn't matter any more. What mattered was that her marriage seemed to be breaking up around her, and there wasn't anything she could do.

She wished desperately she could talk to her parents right now. If she picked up that phone, they'd be there at the other end with help and advice. But how could she admit her marriage was a failure? How could she tell her father that everything he warned about Fred was right?

She remembered his parting words to her, as she and Fred left the wedding reception for the drive south . . . her pale pink going-away dress covered in confetti.

"I've always been honest with you, Maggie," — he always called her that — "so I'm going to be straight with you now. I don't like the bloke. I don't think he's half good enough for my little girl. You should've married Harold. He loves you, and he'd have looked after you. You've broken his heart, y'know. But you're obstinate and you're pig-headed, and I'm to blame for that. It's a family failing. Your grandfather was the same. So take care of yourself, and do what you think best. Your mother thinks I'm being a bit unfair . . . but you know your mother. She thinks love makes the world go around, and perhaps she's right. It's worked all right for us. All I want is for you to be happy."

Then Dan kissed her, shaken hands with Fred, and they'd driven off. She could still remember looking back, seeing her parents, and Max and Tom standing outside in the street, waving to her. She was just twenty then, and began to cry. Fred had put his arms around her, mopped up the tears with his handkerchief, and kissed them away.

Now she was forty, and still crying.

What had happened to the "happily ever after?"

All she had to show for the past twenty years was a husband with a roving eye and no business sense, and two rebellious children.

And this time there was no loving bridegroom to wipe the tears away.

In that empty living room, the proof of Fred's infidelity lying on the floor, Madge wept alone . . .

Chapter 3

CHARLENE and Henry walked down High Street, discussing the scene they'd just escaped from.

"Gee, that was some turn Mum put on there," said Henry. "Wonder what's bugging her?"

Charlene shrugged.

"Who knows? She's in a foul mood today, so it could be anything. I feel sorry for Dad."

Henry wasn't so sure. He knew his mother had a bad temper, but he also knew his father wasn't without his faults. He'd seen him down at the local pub, yarning with his mates, while Madge was working hard at the shop. And he was also aware that Fred had an eye for the women, although he wasn't sure how far it went. Probably not too far. Henry's view was that his father wouldn't be game to cheat on Madge.

Not that Henry was exactly critical of his

dad's fondness for the ladies. The opposite sex also figured high in Henry's life . . . the more, the merrier. He could understand Fred eyeing off a good-looking bird, it was only natural. Like father, like son. But Henry wasn't going to get himself tied down in matrimony and marry young, like his parents. No siree. He intended to go on having a good time for as long as he felt like it — and as long as there were girls, girls, girls . . .

Live for today, and to heck with tomorrow — that was Henry's philosophy.

They were now at the milkbar, where a group of teenage boys were lolling around on the footpath, ogling and whistling any girl passing by. They didn't try it on Charlene, they knew she'd give it as good as she got. Besides, she was Henry's sister, and Henry was one of their mates.

"Hi, Jacko . . . hi, Dakka . . ."

Henry joined the group, as Charlene went inside to meet her girlfriends.

Sitting in one of the booths, already drinking milkshakes, were four of Charlene's classmates from high school. They were Alison Martin (known as 'Big Al'), Helen Kingsley, Jill Turner, and Cynthia ('Cyn') Harrison.

Charlene greeted them, and ordered a double chocolate.

"What's new?" she asked.

Cyn glanced at the others, and then pulled out a double page taken from a magazine. It was a male centrefold, a blonde surfie type with a beach towel strategically positioned.

"Jill reckons she knows he's one of the life-savers from Surfers. She saw him up there last Christmas."

"Yeah," said Jill, a slim brunette. "It's him all right. I recognise the towel."

They all laughed, as Charlene's milkshake arrived and she started drinking it. Chocolate shakes and strawberry doughnuts, they were her favourite foods. She could live on them forever. Luckily she was one of those people who never put on weight, no matter what she ate. Not like Big Al, whose amply proportioned body was always a worry to her — not to mention a source of wisecracks from the boys.

"We're going to put it in Hatch's desk before school on Monday," said Cyn. "Watch her face when she opens it."

Charlene got the giggles thinking about it.

'Hatch' was Miss Hatchett, otherwise known as 'Hatchett-face' to all her students. She taught Maths, and was one of the most unpopular teachers at the school. Most of their spare time was spent thinking up new and outrageous ways to trick or embarrass her . . . preferably without getting caught.

Charlene once put a dead mouse in her hand-bag. But she got caught, because someone told on her. When confronted with the anonymous tip-off, Charlene was too honest to lie about it. Besides, she'd gained considerable prestige among her classmates by thinking it up in the first place. No point in backing off, and pretending it was someone else.

But she'd had to front up to the principal who'd sent a note home to her mother. And Madge hadn't been at all pleased about it. It had led to one of their usual rows, with Madge yelling her head off and cancelling all Charlene's outings and pocketmoney for a month. Luckily her father hadn't been on Madge's side, and had seen the humour in it. Behind Madge's back he slipped Charlene some money. And when Madge thought she was safely in her room doing homework, she'd slipped out the window to meet her friends.

There was a burst of loud laughter from outside the milkbar, where Henry and his mates were still gathered.

"Birdbrains!" commented Charlene contemptuously.

She was fond of Henry, and would stick by him through anything. But she couldn't stand the crowd he was getting around with. No-hopers, all of them, bored out of their minds and just standing around waiting for something to happen. Not one of them had a job. They lived from dole cheque to dole cheque, or what they could manage to scrounge from others.

That won't be me, thought Charlene. She wasn't fond of school, except for the industrial arts classes, and could hardly wait to finish. But she had no intention of lolling around doing nothing, like Henry.

Nor was she interested in doing a business course, like her mother, and working in an office — as so many of her friends had planned to do. The thought of spending eight hours a day indoors, sitting at a desk, wasn't Charlene's idea of fun. She wasn't sure yet what she wanted, but she knew it wouldn't be that. One of her teachers had suggested she look at some of the apprenticeships now being offered to girls . . .

Charlene's dreaming was interrupted by another loud burst of laughter from outside.

"God, what a bunch of dags," said Helen, lighting up a cigarette. She passed the pack around to the others. Charlene shook her head. She'd tried a few times, but decided it cost too much money. She'd rather use it on other things, like buying new discs.

"What'll we do tonight?" asked Cyn.

"Anyone got any ideas?"

"I dunno . . . I've run out of ideas."

"Me too."

"What d'you want to do, Lennie?"

It was Big Al speaking. They all looked at Charlene, waiting for her to come up with something. She thought a moment, then suggested the ice-skating rink.

"I know why she wants to go skating," said Jill. "She heard Ian Kirk say he was going there."

Ian Kirk was the new boy at school. He'd lived in Melbourne, until his parents decided they wanted a warmer climate, and moved north. The move hadn't pleased Ian, he looked on the smaller town as another version of Hicksville. He couldn't wait to get out again, maybe using the excuse of going to university. His parents were well-off, so he knew they'd support him. Meantime, he tried to make the best of a bad job. There were compensations in being new in town . . . country girls not used to slick city ways, were one of them.

Charlene grinned.

"He just said he MIGHT be there. But if he is . . . hands off!"

The four looked at each other, and also grinned.

"Charlene's got the hots for Ian," chanted Big Al.

Cyn looked serious for a moment.

"I hear Jude's after him, and you know what she's like."

"You're gonna have your work cut out, Lennie."

Charlene was openly contemptuous.

"That slag!" she said.

Judy Everingham was sixteen, going on seventeen, but in the same class as the others because she was repeating a year. She wasn't too bright, but what she lacked in brains she made up for in body. All the boys were after her, and rumour was she usually gave them what they wanted.

"Jude's not gonna be at the skating," piped up Helen. "I know, because I heard her arranging to meet Brad Baxter. He's got his dad's car, and they're going to the drive-in.

"Well, that'll leave the field open for the rest of us," said Cyn. She looked mischievously at Charlene, draining the dregs of her chocolate shake. "Might have a go at him myself, I might. He's quite a hunk."

"Out of your league," said Charlene, knowing she was being sent up. "But if you have a go at him, I'll rip your eyes out."

She fished in her purse to see if she had enough money for another shake, then decided she'd better save it for the evening. She might be able to wangle some more out of her father, if he was in one of his good moods. She usually could. On the other hand, after that row with Madge, he might have taken off down to the pub by the time she got home. She wouldn't risk it.

"Will your mum let you out tonight?" asked Jill. "Remember last time, you got into all that trouble."

Charlene was wondering about Madge too, but she didn't want to let on to the others.

"Look, if I say I'll be there . . . I'll be there," she said. "I don't give a stuff what Mum thinks. Just wait for me."

*   *   *

Outside on the footpath, Henry and his friends were getting restless. It had been a full five minutes since anyone worth whistling at had walked by. Two cops cruising past in a police car had paused, and looked at them. It was time to move on.

"Let's go and play some pinball," suggested Dakka. He wasn't born Dakka, his real name was Darryl Andrews. But he considered 'Darryl' to be cissy, so Dakka it was. A young ferret of a kid, he'd dropped out early from school like the rest of them, and now lived on his wits. If they needed a packet of smokes swiped, Dakka was the one sent in to do it. So far he'd managed to dodge the attention of the law, but sometimes he felt his luck could be running out. Like last time, when the shopkeeper caught him. It was only the fact that he was small and wiry, and could run like a greyhound, that saved his skin. Close, but.

"Pinballs!" scoffed Pete Nesbit. "That's for kids. How's about we buy some grog, and then look for some good sorts."

Pete was the biggest of the group, and the oldest. At nineteen, he was a slow-moving loutish figure with thickset features and a swarthy skin. His mother worked as a barmaid, his father was unknown. According to Pete, he was a black American serviceman, down on R. and R. leave from the war in Vietnam. He only guessed, from a snapshot he once found in his mother's handbag. She refused to talk about it.

Jacko (real name Kevin Jackson) cut in. Jacko was the acknowledged leader of the group, and when Jacko talked everyone listened.

"I'm not spending my dough on chicks. Let's just cruise around, and see what comes up."

They started walking down High Street, then turned left. A sign on a white-painted fence church hall proclaimed: NO GOD NO PEACE . . . KNOW GOD KNOW PEACE. They barely glanced at it.

Pete was still buying for grog. They did a quick pool of their resources, and came up with enough for a bottle of Southern Comfort, with a bit left over.

Pete was the one despatched to buy it. They gave him the money, and waited outside. When he emerged, with the brown paper bag in his hand, they went off to a nearby park and had a swig each . . . drinking straight from the bottle.

Henry was more of a beer drinker, but he went along with the rest. The harsh, strong liquor burned his throat as it went down, but it made him feel good. It also made him forget all his problems at home, and the constant squabbles between Fred and Madge over his unemployed state.

The bottle finished, they put their minds on what to do with the rest of the evening. Pete's mind was still on good sorts, and Henry was beginning to side with him. That cute little checkout operator he took out last week, he still had her phone number. It was maybe a bit late to start ringing for a date that same night, but it would be worth a try. And she seemed to fancy him.

Jacko was the one who finally decided it.

"Who's game for a bit of fun?" he asked.

Henry wasn't quite sure what he was talking about.

"What kind of fun?"

Jacko grinned slyly.

"How's about a ride in a nice new Porsche . . . or maybe a Ferrari?"

They all stared at him.

"You gone troppo again?"

Jacko grinned again.

"Of course, if you're too chicken . . ."

Henry knew immediately what he was talking about. Jacko had suggested it before, but somehow they'd never got around to it.

What he was saying is that they should pinch a car, and take it for a joyride. It was not stealing, exactly . . . at least, not in Henry's books. But it still had a lot of risks.

"I reckon we should look for some girls," said Henry.

Jacko had his measure. He knew this was a testing time, and that Henry was popular with the other two. He also knew that if he didn't assert his position as top dog, he would be finished as leader.

"You afraid?" asked Jacko. The question was pointedly directed at Henry.

"Course not," said Henry.

The words sealed his fate.

"How's about you two?" Jacko asked Pete and Dakka.

They nodded assent.

43

"Right, so here's what we do. We cruise around, until we see a likely car. Then Henry here gets into it, he knows how. And we take it for a ride. When it runs out of gas, we dump it. If we see cops around, we dump it anyway and run. Okay?"

Henry had to go along with the others, as they agreed with Jacko.

The Southern Comfort was now beginning to work, and he felt a certain sense of bravado. He could drive, although he'd never bothered to go for a licence. And he liked cars. What harm could it do, borrowing someone's wheels and taking for a spin? It wasn't the same as stealing. The owner would get it back.

Besides, it would look bad if he were the only one in the group to say "no." Jacko could be mean when he liked. All he'd have to do is pass word round that Henry was chicken, and he'd be finished. Finished with the gang, finished with the girls, out in limbo. Nobody liked a wimp.

They started checking the streets and the car parks, looking for a likely car. Something dead easy to get into, something with a bit of style and speed.

As they cruised, Henry began to pick up on the excitement of the others. He thought of putting his foot down on the accelerator, the machine responding to him, the feel of the speed.

And like Jacko said, if there was trouble they could always run.

He only hoped to hell his mother never found out . . .

Chapter 4

MADGE was ironing. She always ironed when she and Fred had one of their periodic blow-ups . . . it helped to soothe her, and put things back into perspective.

Right now she was pressing Charlene's uniform ready for school on Monday. Usually she made Charlene do it. But she wanted to work off some energy, and had run out of shirts and tea towels. Charlene would give her no thanks for it, she knew that. But it made her feel better.

Charlene . . .

She thought back to the time when she was born, back to 1970. It had been a difficult pregnancy, and a difficult birth. Not a bit like having Henry.

Henry had been a joy right from the first moment she realised she was having him. The business was well established, and they were paying off their home. She'd been feeling sick for a couple of weeks, and suspected she might be pregnant. But she wasn't sure, until she went and saw their family doctor.

"Congratulations, Mrs. Mitchell," he'd said. "Come back and see me in a month."

When she told Fred, he was over the moon. He'd broken out a bottle of champagne, and then taken her out for dinner. It had made up for the fact that she'd begun to realise, after only three years of marriage, that Fred had a roving eye.

Madge thought the baby would fix all that. Once it arrived, Fred would realise his responsibilities and settle down to being a good husband and father. And it did, for a while.

Fred was a model parent for the first year of Henry's life. He was caring and sympathetic, when she worked right up to the last week of pregnancy, staggering around the hardware shop and office looking like an overweight elephant. He even told her she looked "lovely."

When they brought her back to the ward, after Henry's birth, Fred was waiting there for her with an enormous bunch of flowers. She felt closer to him than at any time since the early days of their marriage.

Their only argument had been over the name. Madge wanted to call him Jack, after her grandfather. Fred insisted on Henry, after an uncle.

According to Fred, the uncle was rolling in dough and would come good with a bit of money if they named the kid after him. But all they got was a card of thanks. Not even a christening gift.

By that time it was too late to change the name, so Henry it was from then on. And it didn't matter anyway. Whatever the name, Madge loved her firstborn with passion. She spoiled him from the moment he first blinked his blue eyes at her.

When Henry was young, he accepted Madge's love in the way all children accept the love of their parents. But it wasn't long before he realised that he could use it to his advantage. Whenever he got into trouble, Henry knew he could always turn to Madge to get him out of it. All he had to do was turn on the Mitchell charm, and Madge could refuse him nothing.

It was the same charm that had won Madge away from Harold, all those long years ago. And although Fred grudgingly recognised it, and saw in Henry himself at the same age . . . he still felt that Madge was a fool for spoiling their son.

"Making a rod for your own back," he'd constantly say. "Mark my words, that boy means trouble."

It had been a battle to cope with a small child, and help Fred run the business. Sometimes

Madge was so tired at night, that all she could do after dinner was fall into bed.

Their sex life suffered as a result of it. Madge knew she was a disappointment to Fred, and she asked him to be patient. The business was at a critical state, and she needed to put all her energies into making it pay. Madge took Henry to the shop every day, and he slept in a cot in the office.

It was about this time that Fred's roving eye became more than a roving eye, and Madge found out he was having an affair with a neighbour. The neighbour moved soon afterwards . . . Madge never did find out if the husband suspected, or they were moving anyway. But just when she was about to challenge Fred with his infidelity, she discovered she was pregnant again . . . this time with Charlene.

Madge decided, for the sake of the family, to keep quiet and accept Fred's occasional flings. She hoped that having a second child might settle him down. Besides, she knew that walking out on Fred would mean losing eveything she'd put into the business. She had a stake in it now, and was determined not to give up everything she'd worked so hard to achieve.

So Charlene was born, two years after Henry.

She was a breech birth, after a long and painful labour . . . a surprise to Madge, since Henry

49

had come so easily. And she refused to suckle, so Madge had to put her on the bottle.

In a way, it had been a foretaste of what life would be like with Charlene. She was always a rebel, always unwilling to do what was expected of her. Where Henry had been a easygoing and happy child, all smiles and sunshine, Charlene was difficult. Madge would never forget the day Charlene upended a plate of food on Madge's best dress, just as Madge was going to church. And she was only two then.

Yet for some strange reason, Charlene had an instant rapport with Fred. Where he was harsh with Henry, he was like soft butter with Charlene. Sometimes Madge felt he used Charlene's obvious preference for him to get back at her.

The front door opened.

If that's Fred, then I'm going to demand an explanation of the letter . . . thought Madge. She had a right to know.

But instead it was Charlene, rushing into the kitchen to get something to eat.

Madge put Charlene's uniform on a hanger, switched off the iron, and went through to the kitchen to talk to her. Charlene was at the refrigerator, getting out some cold meat and pickles.

Madge noticed, irritated, that there was a tear in Charlene's jeans. And they were the oldest ones in her wardrobe, faded and frayed.

"Why don't you wear something decent for a change," said Madge.

"Like what?" asked Charlene, last night's leg of lamb in one hand.

Like a dress," replied Madge. "Goodness knows I've made enough of them. If you choose to go around looking like a freak, it's not my fault."

Charlene frowned, but didn't answer. She found sometimes it was best to let Madge let off steam. Besides, she'd checked her money again and found out she didn't have enough for the ice-skating. If her father didn't come home in time, she might have to try and wangle some out of Madge. And that was always a problem.

Charlene's silence only irritated Madge more. She was also still upset over the letter she'd found in Fred's pocket, and was taking out her anger and hurt on Charlene.

"Go and tidy up your room, said Madge. "I just went in there, and it's a pigsty."

"So's Henry's," retorted Charlene, her natural rebelliousness getting the better of her resolve to keep on Madge's good side. "He's got more mess than me, but you never jump on him."

Madge did what she always did when she knew she was beaten in an argument . . . she resorted to shouting.

"Don't argue with me, Charlene," said Madge. "Just go and do it."

Charlene sighed, and went off to her room, still eating the leg of lamb.

". . . and don't get grease all over the place. Wash your hands, before you touch anything," Madge called after her.

Left on her own again, Madge began preparations for dinner. Would Fred come home in time to eat with them? Or would he do what he usually did after one of their arguments, stay at the pub and drink with his mates all evening?

Madge knew she wouldn't see Henry until all hours. Once he got in with that crowd of his, roaming around the streets, goodness knows what time he'd come home. Henry was such a restless person, always on the go. A real little livewire, even as a youngster. She remembered the time he'd come home from school, when he was only nine or ten years of age, and he had his schoolbag stuffed with lollies and comics. She'd found them when she went through the bag to see if there were notes from teachers, and asked Henry where he got the money to buy them. Henry had been quite open about it, and said he nicked them from one of the local shops. All the kids at school did it, said Henry. The old geezer who ran the shop was on the grog half the time,

52

and never noticed.

Madge had been appalled, and hauled Henry down to the police station to ask them to give him a lecture. She had lied a bit, to protect Henry, playing down the amount of goods he'd stolen — and saying it was just one small packet of sweets. And she'd said it was the first time — although Henry had admitted he'd been stealing them for months.

The policeman had been kind and sympathetic, complimenting Madge on her handling of the situation. He had given Henry a brief warning, and then given him a tour of the station. Henry had finished trying on a police cap, and charming all the staff. Next day at school he'd bragged about it.

Madge took out some peas, and started shelling them. She was about to put them into a pot, when Charlene burst into the kitchen . . . white with anger.

"What did you do with my blue tee-shirt, the one Cyn gave me?" she demanded.

Madge put the peas in the pot, and calmly started peeling some potatoes.

"If you mean that stinking, filthy thing with ink all over it . . . I thew it out," she said. "It wasn't even worth keeping as a duster."

Charlene was aghast.

"That was my favourite shirt," she

53

said. "Everyone in my class signed their names on it."

Madge's faced tightened.

"So I noticed," she said. "If you think I'd let a daughter of mine go out wearing some of the stuff written on that shirt, then you've got another thing coming. All I can say is that some of the people in your class need their mouths washed out with soap and water.

Charlene's anger was rising.

"That's not the point," she said. "It was my shirt, and you had no right to chuck it out."

Madge made an effort to stay calm. She didn't like these confrontations even more than Charlene did. And she'd had enough trouble for the day.

"I'm only thinking of you, Charlene," she said. "The way you get around, anyone'd think we didn't have two bob to rub together. You know I like to see you in nice things, not that terrible stuff you insist on wearing. What boy's going to fall for someone looking like something the cat dragged in?"

The mention of boys hit a raw nerve with Charlene. She was popular at school, but she was looked on more as a good mate than a femme fatale. She'd always been a tomboy, almost from birth, and played cricket and touch footy with Henry and his friends. Boys liked her, and she was looked on as a fun person. Good old Lennie, you could always depend on her for a laugh.

But so far she'd never had a boy who was special. Someone she could look on as her steady, and say to the other girls "hands off." She'd been kissed heaps of times, and also had a few necking sessions in the back row of the old theatre at Sawtell, a few miles from Coffs Harbour. But unlike some others in her High School class, Charlene was still a virgin.

The hurtful words came out almost before Charlene had time to think of them.

"People in glass houses . . .," she scoffed. "You're a fine one to give lessons in how to hold a man. Nag, nag, nag, that's all you ever do around here. I don't blame Dad for clearing out so he can get a bit of quiet and peace. Why don't you take a look at yourself, before you start giving me lectures."

All Madge's resolves to try and keep some harmony between her and Charlene disappeared in a flash. She knew Charlene felt the problems in her mother's marriage were Madge's fault. But it was hard to stand and take it from a fifteen-year-old.

Madge lashed out, accusing Charlene of always being on her father's side, a traitor to all the hard work and sacrifices Madge had made in bringing her up. Charlene, her temper inherited from Madge, hit back with all the cruel and hurtful things she could think of. They were screaming at each other, saying things that both would later regret. But by that time, it would be too late to take them back.

Finally Charlene had had enough, and stamped off to her room. That's the end of the ice-skating, she thought, as she slammed the door shut. She didn't have enough money, and she was sure now that Fred wouldn't be home for hours. Besides, after that yelling match, she knew that Madge would never allow her out.

Back in the kitchen, a shaken and white-faced Madge picked up a potato and started peeling again. The confrontation with Charlene had upset her more than the one with Fred . . . after all, Charlene WAS her daughter. Could some of those things Charlene said be true? Did she nag too much?

Madge sighed, and tried to put it out of her mind. If Fred came home early, she'd make an effort and be nice to him. Fred and Charlene, both of them carved from the same block of wood, both difficult and prickly to get along with.

Thank goodness, thought Madge, she had a better rapport with Henry. Although she still worried at times about those mates of his . . .

Chapter 5

HENRY and his friends were still roaming around, trying to find a likely car. They split into pairs, taking one side of the street each, but with no luck. Then they decided to try the car park.

Jacko walked through the lanes of cars, surreptitiously testing the door handles as he went past. Suddenly his face brightened.

"Here's one," he said. Henry, Dakka and Pete came over.

The door on the driver's side was locked, but one of the rear passenger doors had been forgotten. Jacko turned to Henry.

"Okay," he said. "Go for it."

Henry was the acknowledged hot-wire expert of the group. Within a minute or two he had the car started, and they all piled into it.

"Good one, Henry," said Jacko.

The car was a new model, red and sleek and gleaming. The tank was three quarters full. Pete

opened the glovebox and checked inside. Sometimes people left spare money in it. No money,
but he found a packet of cigarettes. All except
Henry lit up and started smoking.

Henry, sitting at the back, still had a tight
feeling in his stomach. What would happen
when the owner came back, and discovered his
car was missing? He'd tell the cops for a cert.
Henry was game for almost anything, but he
had sense enough to know that pinching a car
was a bit different from stealing comic books
and lollies.

Then as they headed out of the town, the car
gaining speed, Henry forgot all his worries and
gave himself up to the sheer enjoyment of it. He
could drive himself, although he didn't have a
licence. Fred had given him some lessons, at one
of the rare times when they got along together.
He'd rather have had them from Madge, but
Madge couldn't drive. Fred had tried to teach
her, too, but after two lessons Madge had given
up. She said Fred yelling at her made her too
nervous.

"Give us a go, mate," said Henry from the
rear seat, when they were a few miles out of
town with no one else in sight. Jacko stopped
the car, and Henry changed places with him.

He put his foot on the accelerator, and the car
leaped into action at his touch. It was smooth,

sensitive and responsive . . . just like a beautiful woman, thought Henry.

The thought turned his mind to the rest of the evening. Now if they could just meet some good-looking chicks . . .

"Let's go to Dino's," suggested Henry.

Dino's was a fast food cafe with a winebar. They could hang around the cafe, play the machines, and size up the local talent. And with a car like the one they had, the local talent was sure to be impressed.

The others agreed. Henry turned off at the fork with the burnt-out gum tree, and headed along the country road. It had been a couple of weeks since he'd been out with a girl, and that was a long time for Henry. Who knows, maybe this would be his lucky night.

*   *   *

At home, Madge finished her dinner and looked at the clock. She'd eaten alone, as Charlene had locked herself in her room and refused to talk. Twice Madge had gone to ask if she wanted anything to eat, and twice Charlene had ignored her.

Henry was still out, and so was Fred. Madge toyed with the idea of keeping Fred's dinner

warm on a plate over a saucepan of boiling wat-
ger, and decided against it. If he chose not to
come home, then that was his bad luck. She
scraped the scraps into the kitchen tidy, and
started filling the sink with hot water.

She would do some mending, and then read
that new book she'd just got from the library.
There was nothing much on the telly, Saturday
night was the worst night of the week. Nothing
but sport and old movies.

There was a knock at the front door. Madge
tensed, could it be Fred coming home? Then she
realised Fred wouldn't knock, he had a key.
Madge went to the door, and found her next
door neighbour Beryl standing there. Beryl was
apologetic, she hoped she wasn't disturbing anyone. But she was having trouble with her car,
and wondered if Fred could help? Madge
covered, saying Fred was out on an urgent business call. But she could tell by the look on
Beryl's face that she knew Madge was lying.
How many others in the street knew her marriage was in trouble? Did they gossip about her,
when she went to church on her own on Sundays? (Fred used to go along too, in the early
years of their marriage . . . not so much because
he believed in it, but because Madge insisted.
But had long since given it away, saying it was
superstitious nonsense).

Madge closed the door on Beryl, and picked up her sewing basket. It had been an early birthday gift from Fred — wicker, with a blue satin lining, and compartments for threads and thimble. The satin lining was now worn and faded — like my marriage, Madge reflected. She picked up a pair of Henry's socks, and started darning. Dear, lovable Henry. He may occasionally be a worry to her, but he was the only one in the family who ever put an arm around her, or kissed her. In his own way, he was a good boy.

*   *   *

Henry was having a ball.

He had a girl each side of him, and was trying to decide which one to concentrate on for the rest of the evening. The one on his left was blonde, cute and cuddly, hanging onto his every word and giggling at everything he said. On the other hand, the one on the right, dark-haired and exotic, looked as though she could have hidden depths although she didn't say much.

Pete was in the winebar, chatting up a woman who looked almost old enough to be his mother. He was getting steadily plastered. Dakka and Jacko were at the machines.

"D'you live round here?" Henry asked the brunette. She told him her name was Linda, and she was there on a six month working holiday from Melbourne. Back home, she worked in an office and as a part-time model.

"What do you do?" she asked Henry.

Henry decided to bluff it out. Being on the dole didn't match up with the image of the bright red sportscar.

"I'm with my dad," he said. "We've got a family business."

Linda looked impressed, but didn't ask what kind of business. The cute little blonde giggled, and said Henry hadn't asked about her. But if he wanted to know, she did nails at a beauty salon.

"We specialise in fantasy ones," she said. "You know . . . black with sparkles, initials, anything goofy."

Dakka and Jacko left the machines and rejoined them. Jacko put an arm around the giggly blonde.

"How about we all go for a spin?" he asked, giving Henry a wink. Henry didn't much like the idea of sharing with Jacko. But if he stayed at Dino's with Linda, then he'd have problems getting home.

Pete, staggering on his feet, came back from the winebar. The two girls exchanged glances when they saw him. Then they all went outside to look at the car.

"Six of us in THIS?" asked Linda, as she looked inside it.

"The more the merrier," said Jacko, his arm still around the blonde. "Nice and cosy."

Linda looked again, and pulled the blonde away from Jacko.

"Thanks, but no thanks," she said.

She looked at Pete, his speech now beginning to slur, then at the car again.

"You must think we've got rocks in the head," she said, and walked back into the cafe.

The giggly blonde had one last word for Henry, as Linda dragged her inside.

"Ever want your nails done," she said "ask for Lulu, the first shop on the left."

The four teenagers looked at each other.

"Great," said Henry to Jacko. "The best-looking chick I've met in months, and you blew it for me."

Jacko shrugged.

"So what?" he said. "Let's get back in the car, and see what else we can find."

This time, it was Pete's turn at the wheel.

The alcohol began to take over, as he pushed his foot down hard on the accelerator. The speedo began to climb. Henry was too annoyed about losing out on Linda to even notice.

In a side road just outside the town, a patrol car was waiting. Constable Dawson checked the radar. Another Saturday night speed maniac, ready to add to the road-toll statistics.

As the red car hurtled past, Pete pushing it to its limits, the patrol car took off in chase. Jacko was the first to see it in the rear vision mirror.

"Bloody hell," he said. "We've got the pigs on our tail."

Pete pushed down the accelerator as far as it would go, trying to lose the patrol car. But it kept coming. Henry's mind was now off Linda, and on the problem of eluding the cops. How had he ever allowed himself to be talked into this mess? Taking cars for a joyride was one thing. But he knew that if they ever caught up with the four of them, it would be court and a stealing charge.

Pete tried ducking down a side street, but it was useless. The cops were steadily catching up.

"Okay, let's dump it and split," said Jacko.

Pete braked with such force, that it almost threw the others through the windscreen. Then all four opened the doors, and ran.

Henry was the last one to get out, and sprinted just as the patrol car came to a stop behind them. He hid, shivering, in a side alley, as the police examined the car. Then he ran for his life.

64

"Yeah, this is the one," said Constable Dawson, as he checked the numberplate. "Lucky for the owner, it isn't damaged."

"Do we go after them?" asked Constable Jones, gesturing in the direction of the fleeing teenagers.

"Not worth it," said Constable Dawson. "In the dark, we'd have Buckley's of finding them."

He went back to the patrol car, and radioed to the station. One stolen car, recovered.

"Kids," commented Constable Jones, as he climbed in beside him. "They nick a car for a joyride, and get away with it."

"Maybe not," said Constable Dawson, as he put down his radiophone. "I caught a glimpse of that last one who got out. And I think I know him."

* * *

Madge had just closed her book, and was thinking about getting ready for bed, when Henry came through the front door . . . breathless. She could tell from the look on his face that something had happened, and asked him about it. Henry gave her some story about skylarking around the hamburger shop, and the owner threatening to call the police. A pity he's got no sense of humour, said Henry. Madge agreed — calling in the cops for a bit of youthful fun seemed to her excessive.

She asked Henry if he'd like some hot chocolate, and he said no. But he was hungry, and he'd fix himself a sandwich. Henry went into the kitchen, as Madge gathered up her darning and her book, and prepared to go into her bedroom.

It was then the doorbell went.

Madge answered it, to find a policeman standing there. Two, in fact — she could see another sitting in a patrol car.

"Is this where Henry Mitchell lives?" asked the policeman, introducing himself as Constable Dawson.

Madge tensed, all kinds of warning signals going off in her head. What kind of trouble had Henry got himself into now? In the kitchen, Henry could hear the voices at the front door, and was in a frenzy of panic. Should he go out and give himself up? Or should he lie low, and see what happened. He decided to lie low. It was a wise decision.

Madge immediately went on the offensive. She demanded to know what they wanted to talk to Henry about. Constable Dawson was patient, explaining they'd given chase that night to a speeding car. It turned out to be a stolen vehicle, and the boys concerned had taken off. But as the last one left the car, he thought he recognised Henry.

Constable Dawson reminded Madge he was the one who gave the warning lecture to Henry, when she'd brought him to the station. It had been seven or eight years ago, but Henry hadn't changed that much. Even though it had been dark when the boys ran from the car, he was reasonably certain. And although the kids were probably only joyriding, taking a car was still a serious offence.

Madge seized on those words "reasonably certain" like a drowning man grabs hold of a lifejacket. She told Dawson he was mistaken if he thought he saw Henry. He'd been home all evening with her, and was now in bed asleep.

Listening from the kitchen, Henry went weak with relief. Good old Mum . . . she'd saved his skin once again.

Constable Dawson looked doubtful, but was forced to take Madge's word for it. He apologised for troubling her, and returned to the patrol car.

As soon as the police car drove away, Madge went into the kitchen.

"Right, now tell me the truth," she demanded. "What actually happened tonight?"

Henry told her the truth, glossing over the

67

drinking and the high-speed chase. He said they never intended to steal the car, just take it for a ride and then bring it back. If the owner was stupid enough to leave it unlocked, then that was his problem.

Henry didn't blame his mates, but Madge could read through the lines. She told him he had to stop associating with those hooligans.

Henry protested, saying they weren't hooligans. They were just a bunch of kids like himself, high-spirited and out for a bit of fun. He put his arms around Madge, and nuzzled into her neck.

"You believe me, Mum, don't you?" he asked.

Madge softened, as she always did with Henry. But she kept her voice and expression stern.

"All right, I'll let you off just this once," she said. "But see that it doesn't happen again. I'm warning you, Henry, this is the last time I'll lie for you."

Henry kissed her, and went off to bed.

Madge sighed, looking after him. He was like his father all over again, that Mitchell charm. And against her better judgement, she couldn't resist it. But she was also well aware that Henry had a knack of getting into trouble.

What would he get up to next?

Chapter 6

MADGE tossed and turned in bed, trying to get some sleep. She had so many things on her mind, it was like a dynamo . . . First the business with Fred, and that letter. Then Henry. She had a feeling that Constable Dawson knew she was lying, although there wasn't anything he could do about it. But she knew that from now on, he'd be keeping an eye on Henry Mitchell.

If only Henry would get a job. That was one of of the things she and Fred kept arguing about. Fred considered Henry was lazy, sponging on his family. She kept telling Fred that it wasn't true. Henry was as hard-working as the next one, when he was doing something that interested him. The problem was finding the right kind of job.

Madge tensed, as she heard the front door open.

Fred, shoes in hand, crept into the bedroom.

When he spoke Madge's name, she didn't answer, pretending to be asleep. Fred, relieved, got undressed and fell into bed beside her. There had been nights when he'd come home to find Madge awake and waiting for him — demanding to know where he'd been. He was lucky tonight. He didn't feel in the mood for explanations.

In a minute or two, Madge heard Fred snoring . . . and relaxed. She could smell some other woman's perfume on him, but it didn't worry her like it used to. It still hurt, yes, like a knife twisting in her heart. But she had long since gone past the stage of letting it worry her. Now she just accepted it, as the way Fred was. There would always be other women in his life, she knew that. It was a matter of how long she wanted to put up with it.

In his sleep Fred stirred and put his arm out and touched her. Madge stiffened and lay still, until he rolled back again to the other side.

There had been a time when Fred's touch thrilled her. She could remember when just his fingers on her arm had sent shivers of ecstasy through her body.

Madge thought back to the first time when they'd made love, just a couple of nights after they met.

It had been one of those hot, lazy Brisbane nights.

Her mother had thought she was going to a movie, but Fred had driven them in his salesman's car to a secluded spot by the water. Then he'd taken out a rug, and they'd lain on it close together, looking up at the stars and talking.

Madge was wearing a light, flimsy cotton dress, with her legs bare. Her hair had been longer then, falling around her shoulders. Fred twisted a lock of it through his fingers, as he talked about his plans and hopes for the future — how he didn't intend to be on the road forever, how much he disliked his big, fat boss who was on him like a ton of bricks for every small mistake he made.

"Pig," said Fred. "I do all the work, and he rakes in the dough."

Fred told Madge that as soon as he'd saved up enough money, he was going to move south . . . somewhere smaller, with more opportunities. A country town, maybe. He'd been brought up in the country, and he liked the slower pace.

Madge agreed with him. She told him again about Erinsborough, where she'd spent so much time as a child. It wasn't a town, just an outer suburb of a large city. But it had a small town feel to it. The people there really liked and cared for each other.

As they talked, Fred's hand moved from her hair to her neck, and caressed it lightly. Madge

71

felt the same stirrings she'd had at the dance hall two nights ago, when he'd taken her into his arms. Somehow Fred's touch was ten times more exciting than anything she'd experienced with Harold.

"You're lovely," said Fred, looking down at her in the darkness. Then he kissed her.

What followed had seemed very right and natural at the time. It was only afterwards she felt ashamed and frightened. Fred had been a gentle and considerate lover, knowing Madge's inexperience. She knew she wasn't the first one, but Fred told her she was the first one he'd really cared about. Soon after that, he asked her to marry him.

In the early years, when they moved to Coffs Harbour, the physical side of their marriage had been very satisfying. They were both young, and both had passionate natures. In those days, Fred was too busy establishing his new business to chase after other women.

It was only when he found more free time on his hands, with Madge occupied with raising a family and running the business, that Fred's eye began to wander.

Fred stirred in his sleep and Madge held her breath. She hoped he wouldn't wake up and try to make love to her. Not that he tried too much these days. And when he did, she rebuffed him.

There was too much hurt in her heart for her to be able to respond.

How long had it been . . . weeks? Months? The last time Fred had reached out to her, she'd accused him of coming straight from the bed of another lover. And it probably had been true. But it made Fred very angry, and he'd said cruel things about her being cold and frigid. That also hurt.

Fred began to snore, and Madge relaxed again. When he was snoring, she knew he wouldn't wake up till morning.

She thought of her life as it used to be, and what it was now — empty and pointless. Life was so simple when she was just a kid.

Memories, memories . . .

They kept flooding in on her, as Madge lay awake in bed, staring at the ceiling.

Memories of Ramsay Street, with her brothers Tom and Max, and the good times they used to have. Like the cubby-house they built in the old apple tree out the back, with Tom and Max scouring the neighbourhood for spare pieces of timber, and Madge using Edna's old treadle machine to make curtains for it. Even at that early age, she was always house-proud.

Madge remembered the time she and a couple of her school friends had decided to sleep all night in the tree-house. They'd carried up pil-

73

lows and blankets, and then sat up till midnight talking and eating chocolates. But soon after they settled down to sleep, strange noises started coming from the darkness. They weren't sure what it was, animal or human, but it had them clinging to each other in terror. Then they'd grabbed their pillows, and shinned down the tree-trunk in their nightgowns . . . too terrified to stay there one more minute.

It wasn't until they reached the ground, and found Tom and Max laughing themselves silly, that they realised they'd been tricked.

The wooden cubby-house had been a source of fun for years, and she had pleaded with her parents to be able to take it with them when they moved north. But it wasn't practical to dismantle it and carry it all those miles, so it had finished up as a bonfire for Cracker Night.

Madge could still remember standing there, watching the sparklers and the penny bungers and the catherine wheels, with tears streaming down her cheeks. Dan and Edna had promised her another one as soon as they got to Brisbane. But the new backyard didn't have a tree strong enough to take it. Just Alexander palms, with a couple of mangoes and a papaya. So the tree-house was forgotten.

Until now.

Madge wondered what had brought it back to

her. Maybe it was that feeling of safeness and security she always had as she sat high up in the forked branches, in a green, leafy world of her own. She didn't feel secure now. She felt threatened from all sides, from Fred, from Charlene, even from Henry and his worrying pranks.

If only one didn't have to grow up. If only one could stay a child forever . . . safe, happy, innocent, with life still a wonderful adventure.

Chapter 7

MONDAY morning. Charlene arrived at school, trying to think of an excuse for why she didn't turn up at the ice-rink on Saturday. She knew she could blame Madge for it, and tell about the blazing argument they'd had. All her friends knew she didn't get along with her mother. But some inner kind of loyalty stopped Charlene from talking about it. Although she felt Madge was harsh and oppressive, and couldn't wait until she could leave home, she also didn't believe in airing the family dirty linen in public.

Charlene was still thinking about it, when she ran into Ian Kirk. Literally. She was walking around a corner of the Science Block, when she collided with him and almost fell to the ground.

"Hey, there," he grinned, holding onto her to stop her from falling. Then he looked at her again.

"It's Charlene Mitchell, isn't it?"

Charlene grinned back.

"Lennie to my friends," she said.

They walked together to the quadrangle, where roll call was held every morning. Charlene noticed Cyn and Big Al watching, and felt pleased. Although she'd met Ian Kirk casually a couple of times, he was two classes ahead of her and one of the seniors. In spite of all the talk at the milkbar on Saturday, she looked on him as one of the unattainables . . . remote, to be admired from afar. She knew she didn't stand a chance alongside some of the girls who'd been chasing him . . . girls like Jude, for instance, who was brazen about flaunting her body.

"How're you liking it here?" asked Charlene, as they walked along.

Ian shrugged.

"It's okay," he said. "Bit smaller than my last school. But I can wear it for a year."

"What'll you do then?" asked Charlene.

Ian shrugged again.

"Who knows?" he said. "I'll probably go on to uni. How about you?"

Charlene played it equally cool.

"Probably something like that, too," she said. "Depends on how I go with exams. I dunno, really."

They'd reached the quadrangle, but Ian made no attempt to move away. Although he wouldn't normally bother with one of the juniors, preferring to stay in his own league, there was something about this girl . . . something that combined fresh-faced innocence with a look of devilment. This could be interesting, thought Ian.

From a corner of one eye, Charlene could see that Cyn and Big Al had caught up with them, and were standing nearby watching and whispering. She could guess what they were saying. They were wondering if Charlene was game to follow through with her challenge, and make a play for the new boy. Okay, I'll show them, thought Charlene. I'll get a date with this hunk, if it's the last thing I do.

She flashed a smile at Ian, and moved in closer.

"Been around much since you've been here?" she asked.

"Nope," said Ian, lying. "I'm waiting for a nice girl to show me the sights."

Charlene dazzled with another full-on smile, and looked up at him.

"I'd be very happy to oblige," she said.

Charlene's answer confirmed what Ian had been thinking — this girl was keen on him, and was giving him the green light. She was a bit skinnier than he liked in a girl, a slight little thing with a figure that was almost boyish. But she was blatantly giving him the come-on, her eyes promising untold pleasures.

"How about the drive-in Friday night?" asked Ian. "I can borrow Dad's panel van."

Charlene was impressed. None of the boys in her group were old enough to hold a driver's licence. But she also felt the first twinge of an alarm signal. Going to the drive-in with a boy in a panel van only meant one thing.

She looked over at Cyn and Big Al, who'd been joined now by Jill and Helen. They'd stopped whispering, and were watching her.

Ian was waiting for her answer.

Charlene knew if she turned him down now, she'd never get another chance. He wasn't the kind of guy who'd ask twice. But she also knew that she was venturing into dangerous territory. She decided what the heck, she could handle it. If it got heavy, all she had to do was say "no."

"Sure," said Charlene. "Why not?"

"Where d'you live?" asked Ian. "I can pick you up."

Charlene started to panic. She wasn't sure Madge would even let her out Friday, she'd have to talk her into it. And the last thing she wanted was for Ian to be drawn into a family brawl. It would be too humiliating.

She made some excuse, and arranged to meet Ian in town. He moved off to join some of the older students, and she walked towards her friends.

"Well?" asked Cyn.

"We're going to the drive-in," said Charlene, trying to act cool and nonchalant. "Friday night."

"On wheels or on foot?" asked Big Al. There was a special glassed-in section for moviegoers without cars, or too young to drive them. As the drive-in was the only theatre in town, on weekends it was usually jammed with giggling teenagers.

"He's got a panel van," said Charlene, still trying to play it cool.

"Gee, you're game, Lennie," said Helen. "You wouldn't get me in one of those things for anything. What'll your mum say?"

"What she doesn't know won't hurt her," said Charlene airily. But inwardly, she was worried. What would Madge say if she knew her daughter was going to the drive-in in a sin bin?

"Hope you know what you're doing," said Jill. "What if he puts the hard word on you?"

"He won't," said Charlene, with a confidence she didn't feel. "And if he does, I can handle it."

Just then, she saw Henry passing by outside the school fence. Charlene seized the opportunity to drop the subject of Ian and his panel van,

80

and went over to ask Henry where he was going.

"Mum's been on my back again to get a job," said Henry. "She's been at it all weekend. Reckons if I'm working, it'll keep me out of trouble."

He told Charlene he'd rung the employment agency and was on his way for some interviews.

"Not that it'll make much difference," said Henry. "It'll finish up the same as all the other times — don't ring us, we'll ring you. Sometimes I reckon I should have stayed at school, it'd have made it easier."

"You don't know when you're well off," said Charlene. "Half your luck, not having to swot and do homework. I wish mum'd let me leave."

Henry advised her to stick to it. Every time he went for an interview, and they asked him how much schooling he'd had, he could see from the expression on their faces what they thought: This guy's a dill, no brains. Sometimes it made Henry mad, but there was nothing he could do about it.

"It's all right for you," complained Charlene. "You don't have to work in the store after school. Why don't you ask Mum if you can help Susan in the office? She told me the other day she could do with a hand."

Henry shook his head.

"And have Mum and Dad on my back all the

time?'' he asked. ''They'd drive me mad. Besides that sort of work's all right for a girl. Not for me.

Charlene bridled at the put-down of her sex.

''What d'you mean, all right for a girl?'' she demanded. ''Anything you can do, I reckon I can do better.''

Henry grinned cheekily, at the sudden flare of temper. He could always get a rise out of Charlene.

''Calm down, Lennie,'' he said. ''I was only having you on. But being stuck inside at a desk all day isn't my idea of a job. You know me . . . I'm more the outdoor type.''

''So what do you want to do?'' asked Charlene.

''Make a million, then sail around the world with an all-girl crew,'' said Henry.

Charlene laughed. She could never stay mad at her brother for long.

''Good luck with your interviews,'' she called out, as Henry walked on.

Chapter 8

"A FAMILY DIVIDED"

HENRY was at his fourth and last interview. He was getting tired of walking around the town, getting knockbacks. All the others had worked out as he thought they would . . . a brief questioning, then a polite "thanks", and the information that they needed someone with more qualifications or experience.

Henry was beginning to get annoyed, in spite of himself. He wasn't that keen on finding a job. On the other hand, it was irritating to be turned down all the time because of lack of experience. How was he expected to get experience if no one would give him a job?

Henry looked at the address on the piece of paper in his hand, and at the building he was standing outside. ACE MANUFACTURING PTY LTD. Yeah, this was the one.

He went inside the building, and walked up to the girl at the reception desk, asking for the personnel manager.

"It's Mr. Quinton," she said. "First door on the right, upstairs."

Henry lingered a moment, turning on the charm. The receptionist was young and very pretty, and he had a feeling she liked him. If he got the job, working there could have its advantages.

"Been here long?" he asked.

"I only started last week," said the receptionist.

"Tell you what," said Henry, flashing a smile. "If I get the job, how about I take you out to lunch tomorrow?"

She smiled, and Henry noticed her eyes were a greenish-blue.

"It's a date."

Henry looked at the piece of paper again and started to climb the stairs. The agency said the job was for a packer and storeman. Hard work, but he didn't mind that.

"Good luck," the girl called out from the desk. Henry gave the thumbs-up signal, and grinned back at her. Yes, she had decided possibilities.

At the top of the stairs, first right, was a glass door with the words on it: B.W. QUINTON, Personnel Manager. He knocked, and went in.

B.W. Quinton turned out to be a large, heavy man in his forties, balding and wearing glasses.

He looked over the top of them at Henry, as he eased inside the door with the piece of paper still in his hand.

"Yes, boy," he asked.

Henry didn't like that "boy" bit. He had the feeling he didn't like Mr. Quinton. But this was his last chance for the day, and he wanted to make a good impression. If he went home, and once again had to admit failure, he knew what would happen. Madge would carry on, wanting to know why he didn't get the job, what he'd done wrong, what people had said to him, what he'd said back to them. And Fred would just make some sour comment to the effect of "what d'you expect?" The lad's a failure, he'd say to Madge. He doesn't amount to tuppence, and never will. Adding, as he always did . . . but of course, you spoil him.

Henry explained he'd come for a job interview, and who had sent him. Mr. Quinton gestured at a chair, and told him to sit down.

"What's your experience?" he asked Henry.

Henry's heart sank. This interview wasn't starting out too well. He mentioned a couple of part-time jobs, such as gardening and stacking supermarket shelves. Mr. Quinton didn't look impressed.

"References?" he asked, holding out his hand.

85

Henry explained they'd only been part-time jobs, and he hadn't asked for a reference. What he didn't say was that he'd been fired from both . . . the gardening job because he'd taken all day to weed a couple of flower beds, and at the supermarket he'd spent too much time chatting up one of the check-out girls. When the manager came to inspect his work, he found Henry had put all the washing powders on the shelves reserved for breakfast cereal. It was hello and goodbye pretty fast at that job, Henry remembered.

"School report?" was the next question from Quinton. Henry was hoping he didn't have to answer this one. He said he thought the job involved storeroom work, packing and loading on to trucks. He didn't realise there was anything required other than muscle.

"We like all our staff to have a reasonable level of education competence," said Mr. Quinton pompously. "That way we can switch them to other duties if necessary. Your school report, boy."

Henry reluctantly took out the folded and well-thumbed piece of paper. It was from his last year at school, when he was fifteen, and the report hadn't been a good one. There were some marks that weren't bad, like English — which he enjoyed. But at the end of the report was that damning comment: "Henry could do better if he concentrated more. Class behaviour is often disruptive."

Quinton frowned as he looked at it, then handed it back.

"You Fred Mitchell's son?" he asked.

Henry nodded. Coffs Harbour wasn't that big a town, and most of the business people knew each other. He wasn't sure if being Fred Mitchell's son was going to be a good thing or not. He soon found out.

"Sold me some crook paint once," said Quinton. "Bloody stuff ran down the walls first time it rained. Wrecked all my flower beds."

Henry knew at that moment he wasn't going to get the job.

Quinton walked him to the door, and saw him out.

"We've got some others to interview," he said. "Don't raise your hopes, sonny boy. Just leave your name with the girlie at the front desk."

He paused, as Henry was about to leave. For a moment Henry wondered if he was still thinking about the crook paint, and was going to ask for his money back.

"Want a bit of advice from an old hand?" asked Quinton. Henry didn't, but he knew he was going to get it.

"Get off your backside and roll your sleeves up. Start from the bottom, boy, and get some experience."

Henry didn't bother to leave his name at the front desk. When the pretty receptionist asked how he'd gone, he shrugged and gave her the thumbs down. She didn't mention lunch.

Outside, Henry ripped up the piece of paper and threw it away. He felt like ripping up that school report as well, but decided against it. Maybe some day it would come in handy.

As he turned the corner, he ran into Jacko.

"Hey, why the poncy gear?" asked Jacko.

Henry's clothes weren't exactly fancy, but they were a bit better than the ones he usually wore around the streets. Madge had insisted, and had even bought a new shirt for him.

Henry explained about the job interviews, and how they'd turned out. Jacko was openly contemptuous.

"You're a mug, you need your head read," he said. "Working your guts out for a few lousy bucks a week. There're easier ways to make money."

"Like what?" Henry asked him.

Jacko sidled closer, and lowered his voice. He looked around to see if anyone was nearby listening.

"Like getting into a warehouse," he said.

Henry wasn't sure at first what Jacko meant. Jacko explained he was talking about pulling off a robbery. It would be as safe as houses, he told Henry. They would pick some place easy to break into, and then nick a few things. Maybe something with electrical goods, so they could get a few videos. Stuff that was easily sold in the back streets and pubs, and fetched some quick money.

"You're nuts," said Henry. "I'm not getting into anything like that. What if we get caught?"

"We won't be," said Jacko, supremely confident. "We'll pick some place that isn't patrolled . . . I know one that's dead easy. Like getting into a sardine tin."

For a moment, Henry was tempted. It sounded like a dead easy way to make some money, and Henry could do with extra cash right now. He'd spent most of his dole cheque on Saturday night, and was now down to a few dollars.

Then he decided against it. He wasn't nearly as confident as Jacko about them getting away with it. Also, taking cars for a joyride was one thing. Breaking and entering was another. Henry might be wild at times, but what Jacko was suggesting was too heavy . . . even for him.

"Please yourself," shrugged Jacko. "If you're too chicken . . ." And he walked on.

Henry knew he'd gone down a few notches in Jacko's estimation. Jacko was the natural leader of their group, and most of the time Henry fell in with his plans. But this was one time that Henry wasn't prepared to follow blindly. He had a feeling Jacko would eventually end up in jail, and he didn't particularly feel like joining him there.

Henry wondered what the reaction of the others would be to Jacko's suggestion. Probably the same as his, he thought. Although Dakka might be talked into doing it, he enjoyed something with a bit of risk to it. And Pete was too stupid to know.

Henry was still thinking about what Jacko said to him, when he ran into Linda, the girl he'd met at Dino's.

"Hi," she said. "Small world."

Henry's mood perked up immediately. Linda was wearing some kind of red clinging dress, and looked gorgeous. And she looked very pleased to see him.

"Where's the car?" she asked, looking around. Henry had almost forgotten about that.

"I left it home today," he said. "Too many hassles parking."

He made a mental check of how much money he had, and decided he had enough for two soft drinks.

"Got time for a Coke?" he asked. Linda said she had plenty of time. She'd got bored at the place where she was staying, and had decided to come into town for the day. Look around the shops, maybe buy a few souvenirs.

"Great," said Henry, steering her by the elbow towards the nearest milkbar, "Something fell through, and I just happen to have the day free myself."

They settled themselves into a booth, and Henry ordered the two drinks. At second meeting, Linda was even more attractive than the first. And this time he had her to himself.

"Gee, I'm pleased I ran into you," she was saying. "This must be my lucky day . . . you've no idea how bored I was feeling."

Henry grinned, as he paid for the drinks. He knew he only had a dollar left, but he'd find some way around it. Maybe call in at the store, and see if he could talk Madge or Susan into advancing him some petty cash.

"My lucky day, too," said Henry, as he took Linda's hand and smiled at her. Linda smiled back.

Every cloud has its silver lining, thought Henry. It had been a lousy day so far, with all those interviews and knockbacks. But running into Linda had changed his luck. Things were finally starting to look up . . .

Chapter 9

"A FAMILY DIVIDED"

FRIDAY night. For the first time in ages, all four Mitchells were sitting around the dinner table together. And the mood, although not exactly one of happy family warmth, at least seemed to be free from arguments. More like an armed truce.

Madge wondered idly what had put Fred in such a good mood, and why he'd come home early instead of going to the pub to drink with his mates for an hour or two. Usually he did this on a Friday night, after checking through the books and the cash with their office secretary Susan Cole. This time, he'd come straight home.

Charlene was quiet, thinking of her date with Ian. She'd arranged to meet him outside the Civic Centre. But she still hadn't told her parents, unsure of their reaction. Madge, in particular, wouldn't be pleased about it. Last time she'd gone, she'd had to battle all afternoon . . . and Madge finally only agreed, when she knew she was going with a group. Charlene decided the best tactic was to bide her time, and then try to slip it into the conversation without drawing too much attention to herself.

Henry gave her the opportunity. He announced he was taking Linda to a movie at Sawtell. That was fine with Madge. He'd brought Linda into the store when he came to borrow some money the other day, and Madge thought she seemed a nice girl. Quiet and refined, not like some of the floosies he sometimes took out. Madge would like to see him meet a nice girl, and settle down to going steady. Someone ladylike, who would also encourage him to get a job and earn a living. Madge remembered how she'd encouraged Fred in those early days. When they first came to Coffs Harbour, she'd been the one who pushed Fred into his own business. And she'd been pushing him ever since. Left to himself, Madge knew that Fred would never have got anywhere. Too lazy, for one thing. And too fond of throwing around money. That's what Henry needed, someone like herself who would make him more responsible. And Linda could be the one.

Henry turned to his father.

"Don't suppose you could lend me some money?" he asked. "Just until my next cheque comes through."

Fred's good mood vanished, and his face hard-
ened.

"Fat chance," he said. "Not until you pay
back the money you've already borrowed from
petty cash. Susan told me all about it. Bloody
nerve, coming in like that.

Madge tried to defuse the situation.

"I authorised it, don't blame Susan," she said,
adding hastily: "I meant to put it back out of my
own pocket, but forgot."

"Yeah," sneered Fred. "Covering up for your
son, as usual."

Funny how it was always "your son" whenever Henry got into trouble, thought Madge, and
"my son" on the rare occasions when Henry did
something right. Like the time he'd won a
school medal for running.

Henry knew he had no chance of getting any
money out of his father. But he was in a spot,
because he'd already arranged to meet Linda.
Madge saw the look on his face, and patted his
hand.

"Don't worry," she said in a low voice. "I'll
lend you some."

Charlene overheard, and decided this was a
good time to slip in a mention of her own date. It
irritated her sometimes that Madge favoured
Henry so much. Like offering to pay for his date
tonight. Charlene could just imagine what

would happen if she asked Madge the same thing. Still, this was no time to stew over the unfairness of life. At least Henry had given her the perfect opening to broach the subject of Ian.

"I'm going out too," she said.

Madge looked sharply at her.

"Who with?"

"You don't know him," said Charlene. "He's new at school . . . Ian Kirk."

Charlene was hoping Madge wouldn't ask where she was going, but she was out of luck. It was the first thing Madge wanted to know. When Charlene told her the drive-in, Madge exploded.

"No daughter of mine's going to a drive-in with a boy I don't even know," she said. "Don't think I don't know what goes on there, I've got ears. Any boy who takes a girl there's only out for one thing."

Charlene sighed. This was going to be tougher than she thought.

"You've got the wrong idea, Mum," she said. "It's not like that at all. He's just new in town, and he asked me out . . . that's all. Don't make a big thing of it."

Madge knew she was starting to sound like a harridan, but she couldn't help herself. There was something about Charlene that always brought out the worst in her.

95

"If you want to go to a movie, go with Henry and Linda," she shouted.

Henry and Charlene looked at each other. Neither wanted to double date. But how could they get this across to Madge, when she was in one of her screaming tantrums?

Fred intervened, to come in on Charlene's side.

"I can't see why you're making so much fuss, Madge," he said mildly. "What's the harm in the girl going to a drive-in?"

Madge switched her anger to her husband.

"You wouldn't," she said. "Not when you've got the morals of an alley cat. Any time I try to show my daughter what's decent, you like to aggravate me by coming in on her side."

Henry decided it was a good time to escape. He left the table, and went to his room to change. He was by nature peaceful, and didn't like confrontations. When Madge and Fred started one of their many arguments, Henry tended to switch off and move out.

Charlene and Madge were still glaring at each other.

"I'm going, and you can't stop me," said Charlene. She stormed off to her room.

Left alone at the dinner table, Fred and Madge sat looking at each other. Fred was already regretting that he'd decided to come

96

home early tonight. Perhaps he should have gone to the pub after all? Or asked Susan out for a meal. She'd been a very sympathetic listener, when he was telling her some of his marriage problems. Now there was someone who knew how to handle a bloke, not like Madge who nagged him all the time. And he had a feeling she liked him. It was because he'd driven her home, only a block away, that he'd decided to come straight home for dinner. He was still thinking about Susan when Madge resumed the attack on Charlene.

"Typical," she said. "You don't care what happens to your daughter. Why should you, it didn't worry you twenty years ago.

"What're you on about?" asked Fred.

"I tell you what I'm on about," said Madge. "I'm talking about the time I let you sweet-talk into you-know-what. Two nights after we met, that's what I'm on about."

Fred started to get angry.

"I don't remember you complaining," he said. "Takes two to tango."

Madge was fit to blow a fuse.

"That's great," she said. "Blame me for it. I was just an innocent girl, and you know it. You seduced me. And we were both lucky that I didn't get pregnant. Well, I don't want Charlene to go through the same thing."

97

Fred got up and walked out. He paused at the door, and looked back.

"I should've left you with that nincompoop whatsisname . . . Harold."

*　　*　　*

Charlene was dressed, ready to meet Ian Kirk. Although she wasn't normally that interested in clothes, she'd taken special pains tonight — a frilly, white off-the-shoulder cotton blouse, a blue denim skirt, sandals. Those words of Madge's about the way she looked still rankled with her. So far Ian had only seen her in her school uniform. She'd show him tonight she could look as nice as the next girl.

She was applying eye makeup, and trying to decide which earrings would look best, the gold hoops or the purple plastic, when Madge came in.

"Where d'you think you're going?" said Madge.

Charlene stiffened.

"I told you, I've got a date."

"And I told you," said Madge "that I'm not letting you go to a drive-in with a complete stranger."

Charlene threw up her hands in despair.

"For heaven's sake, he's not a stranger. He's a boy at school. And there's nothing going to happen, nothing. All we're doing is going to see a movie."

"All right," challenged Madge. "Then tell me what movie you're going to see."

She had Charlene there. Charlene hadn't the faintest idea what the program was. But she made a wild guess.

"Wrong," said Madge. "That was last month. I remember reading it in the paper. Now admit it, the only reason you're going is because it's a chance for some hanky panky in the back seat. And even if you don't respect yourself, I'm going to make sure you don't get a chance to get into trouble. You're staying home."

Charlene turned white with anger.

"I'm going, and you can't stop me," she said. It was the worst possible thing to say to Madge, who was still smarting from the confrontation with Fred.

"Oh, can't I?" she said.

She slammed out, and turned the key in the lock.

"This room's the only place you'll be going tonight, my girl," she said and stomped off.

Charlene hammered at the door for a few minutes, shouting at Madge to let her out. Then when she realised Madge was serious, she sat on her bed and started thinking what to do.

Madge was determined not to let her go to the drive-in, that much was very clear. But Charlene knew that if she didn't turn up to meet Ian, it would be the last time he would ever ask her out. There were plenty of other girls who'd jump at the chance of a night at the drive-in with the spunkiest boy in the school. It had been sheer luck he'd asked her in the first place, if she didn't show, it would be goodbye Ian.

Charlene decided to defy her mother, and go. The most she would be in for would be another screaming match when she got home, and she was used to those. But she'd been bragging all week to the other girls about the drive-in date, and to pull out now would be an ignominious retreat. She'd never live it down.

Charlene checked the window, and then put her eye to the door. She could hear Madge in the living room, and the telly on. Charlene turned on the radio. Then she grabbed a jacket and her handbag, and climbed through the window. The light was on in the living room, and she could see Madge through the curtains. Charlene crept past, and then ran down the road. With a bit of luck, she could still make it to the Civic Centre in time.

*   *   *

"What's the matter?" Ian asked.

They were at the drive-in, parked in the last row. Ian had been talking to her, but Charlene hadn't heard what he was saying. She was still thinking about Madge, and wondering what she'd do if she found out Charlene had gone.

"Nothing," said Charlene, dragging her mind back to the movie. It was one of those hot, steamy stories, and the hero and heroine were now in bed with each other. There was a flash of bare breast, as they moved into each other's arms.

As Charlene tried to concentrate on the story, Ian moved in closer and put his arms around her. Then he kissed her, a long, passionate kiss. Charlene resisted automatically at first, and then responded. After all, wasn't this the whole reason why she'd come out with him in the first place? This was the kind of thing she could brag about to the other girls on Monday morning . . . having Ian Kirk, the school hunk, all to herself in the front seat.

All around them, other couples were locked in passionate embraces, or had disappeared completely into the backs of cars and panel vans. The on-screen heavy breathing was being matched by the heavy breathing of dozens of red-blooded teenagers, out for their one big night of the week.

"Let's go in the back," said Ian, tugging at Charlene.

Charlene hesitated, knowing what could be ahead. She had nothing against sex, and knew it would happen to her one day. But she wasn't sure if this was the right time. Years of Madge drumming into her that "nice girls don't do it," and warnings about "giving in too easily," had had their effect. One part of her was fired with the excitement of doing something adventurous and forbidden. Another part of her felt afraid and guilty, as though Madge were in that panel van with them, watching.

"Come ON," whispered Ian, pulling her into the back. "What's wrong, you afraid or something? If you are, then we'll go home."

Charlene pulled herself together, and climbed in the back with him. There was already a blanket on the floor, and a couple of cushions. Ian pulled out a hip flask, and offered her a drink. It was the first time Charlene had tried spirits, and the raw, strong taste burnt her throat going down. But it also calmed her fears and she stopped trembling.

"That's more like it," said Ian, as he had a drink himself, and then pulled her close to him. He kissed her again, more passionately than before, and his hand reached under her skirt.

Charlene pulled away and sat up. Everything

was happening much too fast for her and she needed time to think.

"What's wrong now?" asked Ian. He was starting to sound irritated.

Careful, careful . . . thought Charlene. She didn't want to antagonise him. On the other hand, she also didn't want to let him know this was the first time for her. What a country hick he'd think she was! He'd already made his feelings clear about sóme of the girls he'd been with since he moved north. And she knew from hearing him talk that most of the ones he dated were already experienced.

Charlene shut her mind to the warning signals, and lay down on the rug again. Ian was far and away the most sophisticated boy she'd ever known, and she meant to make the most of it.

She tried to forget her mother, but Madge's voice kept drumming through her head — criticising the way she looked, the way she talked, her tomboy clothes and habits. You'll never catch a boy, Charlene . . . never catch a boy . . . never . . .

When Ian's hand crept up her thigh again, she didn't pull away this time or protest. She just shut her eyes and gave in to him, trying to relax. But when it was over, she lay there feeling nothing, wondering . . . is that all there is? All she felt was dirty, dejected. As Ian took another swig from the hip flask, tears welled in Charlene's eyes.

Driving back later, Ian asked how she was feeling. If he guessed the truth about her, he didn't let on. He let her out a block from her house, and waved a casual goodbye. Not even a goodnight kiss.

"See you around, Lennie," he said.

Charlene knew then it was all over. She'd known from the start that he was taking her to the drive-in for one thing, but it still hurt to realise the truth. She felt used. If only he'd shown her some small sign of affection. Just a sign he liked her for herself . . .

Charlene stood and watched the tail lights of the panel van disappear around the corner, and started walking slowly to her home. Funny how everything could change so much in a few hours. This morning, going out with Ian Kirk had seemed the greatest thing in the world. Now all she was beginning to feel was a burning anger — at Ian Kirk — at herself.

Chapter 10

As Charlene lay in bed trying to get up but knowing that when she did she'd be sick again, she knew beyond any doubt that she was pregnant.

She tried swinging her leg to the floor, and willing her mind to think of something else. Maybe if she moved very slowly, taking it easy, the feeling of nausea would go away. Please, just this once.

But it didn't. As soon as she stood up and walked over to get her dressing-gown, it came over her in waves. Charlene couldn't stop herself, she just had to grab a towel and rush for the bathroom.

In the bathroom, she locked the door and threw up, trying to keep as quiet as possible. Fortunately this time Madge would be in the kitchen cooking breakfast. Breakfast . . . The very thought of it made Charlene heave and throw up again. Then white and shaking, she sat on the edge of the bathtub and tried to pull herself together.

Henry was knocking on the door, demanding to know how long she'd be. He wanted to get out of the house early, and look for a job again — not because of Madge's constant badgering, but because he'd asked Linda to a ball next month. And he needed money in a hurry to pay for it.

"I'll only be a minute," Charlene called out. She ran the shower quickly, and got under it. As she showered, she looked down at her slim, almost boyish body. She'd always been the envy of her school friends, because no matter how much she ate she never put on an ounce in weight. Big Al was always at her about it.

"Lucky Lennie," Big Al would say. "You never have to worry about dieting. Me, I only have to look at a doughnut sideways, and it puts an inch on my hips."

Charlene was trying to imagine herself fat, and couldn't. But in a few months she'd be just like those large, clumsy pregnant women she saw staggering around the supermarkets. What could she do? Who to turn to? Not her mother, that's for sure. If Madge knew the truth, she'd kill her.

Henry was banging on the door again, shouting for Charlene to hurry up. She dried quickly, put on her dressing-gown again, and came out.

"What's the idea of locking yourself in?" asked Henry, as she emerged. "Think someone's going to perv on you, or something?"

Normally Charlene could take Henry's jokes in her stride. But she wasn't herself this morning — she was too tense and worried by the secret she was hiding.

"Drop dead," she snapped, and walked back to her room. Henry looked after her, surprised, then shrugged and went into the bathroom.

Back in her room, Charlene began to dress for school. She was always a slow starter in the mornings, in fact it was a family joke that Charlene never woke up until she'd had her orange juice. But this morning, she was even slower than usual. She wished desperately for it to be a weekend, so she could crawl back beneath the covers and stay in bed. But it was Monday, and she had to front up to both her family and friends.

Friends . . .

Charlene thought back to the Monday six weeks ago, after the night at the drive-in with Ian Kirk. She'd gone to school, still feeling angry with herself for giving in so easily, but hoping at least Ian would say something. Just a word, a friendly gesture, anything to make her feel not so cheap. She didn't regret what happened in

the back of the panel van. But she was beginning to feel Ian had just used her. If only he'd
phoned next day, or showed some sign he liked
her as a person.

But the phone never rang. And when she saw
him with a group of High School friends in the
main street, he'd turned away and pretended he
hadn't seen her. At first Charlene made all kinds
of excuses for him. Perhaps he hadn't seen her.
Or he didn't want to let his mates know he'd
dated one of the school juniors. Maybe when she
got to school on Monday, he'd come over and
talk to her. Just some indication that he was still
a friend.

But he never did. Instead, Cyn had asked her
was it true what Ian was boasting? When Charlene demanded to know what she was talking
about, Cyn had told her it was all around the
school. Ian had bragged that Charlene was a
pushover, a real hot little number. Cyn was all
agog for details. Charlene felt something die inside her, there and then. She lied, telling Cyn
that Ian was just trying to get back at her for
refusing him. He'd tried it on, said Charlene,
and she'd walked out on him and gone home.
He might be the school hunk, but she was one
girl he couldn't have on a plate. Cyn was sympathetic, and so were other friends. They all
agreed Ian was a real pig. That's the trouble

with boys, they said, getting together in a huddle to talk. Get on the wrong side of them, and they can spread any story they like. It's not fair. And half the time, it's just because they want to look good with their mates. Protecting the male ego, just because they don't want to admit they've had a knockback.

So her friends rallied around, even if they didn't believe her. It was the battle of the sexes — Us against Them. Eventually Charlene put that night at the drive-in out of her mind, and even managed to walk past Ian in the school ground without feeling hate. It's over, she told herself.

But it wasn't over. At first she ignored the signs, refusing to believe what they were telling her. But as she started to feel sick morning after morning, she knew she had to face up to the truth.

*　　*　　*

"What's up with you, Charlene?" asked Madge. "You've hardly touched any of your breakfast."

Charlene looked down at the bacon and eggs, feeling the nausea rising again. She pushed it away, saying she didn't feel very hungry. All she wanted was a piece of dry toast. Henry grabbed her plate, piling the food on to his.

"Thanks, Lennie," he grinned. "All contributions gratefully received."

Charlene tried to manage a smile, but it was an effort. Madge looked at her, concerned. Was Charlene going through some silly dieting fad, trying to stay thin? Or was she sick, and should see a doctor?

Charlene tensed, at the mention of the word 'doctor'. He was the last person she wanted to face right now.

"I'm okay," she said. "Just not feeling hungry, that's all."

"And you weren't hungry yesterday, or the day before that," said Madge, her mood changing from concern to irritation. "Beats me what gets into you at times, Charlene. I go to a lot of trouble to make sure you go off to school with a good breakfast, and then you won't eat it. Next time, just tell me before I waste my time cooking it."

Fred looked up, frowning.

"Why don't you get off the kid's back?" he said. "She says she's all right, she's all right. Leave her alone."

"And what would you know?" demanded Madge, turning on Fred. "Half the time you're not home. You wouldn't know if one of your

110

children were dying right under your nose.''

"Come off it," said Fred, starting to get angry. "All the girl's done is say she's not hungry. The way you're talking, you'd think she had one foot in the grave.''

"That's right, take Charlene's side as usual," said Madge. She knew she was starting to shout again, but she couldn't help herself. Somehow these days, even the simplest family conversation ended up in an argument. She knew she was nervy, and that things irritated her more than they should. But constant worrying about Fred's infidelity, wondering which woman he was sleeping with now, were beginning to take their toll. I'll have to pull myself together, thought Madge. I mustn't go to pieces.

Charlene and Henry decided to escape the bickering — Charlene because she was still feeling queasy, and Henry because he was anxious to start his job-hunting. If he couldn't make some money, the date with Linda would be off. He knew her type. She liked him, he was certain of that. But she was also the kind of girl who expected to be taken out in style. He would have to borrow a car for the ball, and try to make up some reason why he no longer had the sleek red sports model. And then there was the cost of the tickets, and the hire of a monkey suit. He wouldn't see much change out of a hundred bucks.

Henry knew his father wouldn't help him, and he was reluctant to try Madge again. He still owed her money from the last time. Maybe Charlene had something tucked away for a rainy day? She had a bank account, he knew. But knowing Charlene, there probably wasn't much in it.

Henry knocked on Charlene's door.

"Who's there?" called Charlene. Her voice sounded strange, muffled and thick, as though she'd been crying. When she realised it was Henry, and not Madge, she let him in.

"Anything wrong?" Henry asked, looking at her red-rimmed eyes. Although they were good friends, Lennie was sometimes hard to figure out. She was like Madge in a way, subject to quick mercurial changes of mood. On a high one minute, and down in the depths the next. He wondered if she were having boy trouble. Maybe it was that guy she went to the drive-in with, Ian Whatshisname. He knew Madge had forbidden her to go, but one of his mates had seen her there. Lennie hadn't talked about it afterwards, which was a bit strange. Usually she told him everything.

"Nothing's wrong. What d'you want?" asked Charlene.

Henry told her about the date with Linda, and his urgent need for some cash in a hurry. Could

Lennie help out? He'd pay her back as soon as he found a job, he said. It was just that the tickets were selling like hot cakes, and if he didn't buy them soon he could miss out. A hundred bucks would see him over the emergency.

"A hundred bucks . . . you must be joking," said Charlene.

"Fifty?" tried Henry.

Charlene could feel the sickness coming over her in waves again, and just wanted to get rid of Henry so she could be miserable on her own.

"Look," she said testily. "I haven't got that kind of money, even if I wanted to help you. So rack off . . . I've got my own problems."

Henry moved towards the door, then paused a moment.

"What kind of problems?" he asked.

For a moment, Charlene toyed with the idea of telling him. Henry would be kind and sympathetic, she knew that. But she also knew how close he was to Madge, and she couldn't be certain he wouldn't tell — out of concern for her. And Madge blowing her top was something Charlene didn't feel like coping with right now. No, there had to be another way.

"Forget it," she said. "Just a few hassles at school, that's all."

Henry left, and Charlene held a towel tightly over her mouth, trying not to throw up. Then

the wave of nausea over, she began to get ready
for school.

*   *   *

"Hi, Lennie, how's the weekend?"

Cyn, Big Al, Jill and Helen were waiting for
her at the school gates when Charlene arrived.
Usually the five of them knocked around together on the Saturday, and then talked on the
phone to each other Sundays. But Charlene had
begged out for the past few weeks, her excuse
being that Madge wanted her to help out at the
shop.

As they walked along towards the quadrangle, Ian Kirk passed them with a blonde on his
arm, looking at him and giggling at something
he'd said.

Cyn glanced at Charlene, trying to gauge her
reaction. Charlene, frozen-faced, walked on
with no comment.

"I know that girl," volunteered Big Al, trying
to be kind and spare Charlene's feelings. "She's
a dag, my brother went out with her once. Reckoned she had nothing upstairs, she was real
dumb. He never asked her out again. Name's
Julie. Don't know what he sees in her, she's not
a patch on you, Lennie."

114

"Yeah, you'd run rings around her any time," said Jill.

Charlene knew they were trying to be nice to her, and make her feel better about the way Ian had dumped her after one date. They were like that, her friends. Any time there was a crisis, they rallied around each other . . . protective as mother hens. Normally she'd appreciate their efforts, and thank them for it. But she was too worried about what to do about her pregnancy to be able to respond.

Again, as with Henry, she toyed with the idea of confiding the truth. She knew they'd be loyal, and stick with her. But her commonsense also told her there was nothing they could do to help. Sympathy was no use, right now she needed some practical advice from someone a bit older. All she knew was she couldn't go through that pregnancy, and have the baby.

The conversation turned to what they'd do after school. Cyn suggested they all hang out at the milkbar, and see what happens. Saturday night she'd met a boy there, a mechanic from one of the local garages. He had his own car, and had taken her for a drive in it. Nothing much had happend, but he seemed pretty keen. She'd told him she usually went to the milkbar after school, and she had a feeling he could turn up again. And he had a hunky friend who

115

worked in the same garage, she told Lennie.

Usually this would be enough to have Charlene drop everything, and go with her friends. She was mad about cars, and couldn't wait until she was old enough to get her licence and drive one. Sometimes Fred let her help him, when he was tinkering around fixing the engine. Madge didn't like her doing it, complaining of grease all over her clothes, and having to scrub her fingers to the bone to get them clean again. Fixing cars was men's work, thought Madge, who wouldn't have a clue what went on under the bonnet anyway.

But this time Charlene didn't feel in the mood for hanging around, and having to make conversation with strangers. She told them Madge had ordered her to come straight home, and give a hand at the hardware store. And this time she wasn't making it up. As she was leaving that morning, Madge had told her she was going to be tied up all afternoon with some committee or other. Usually at times like that, Fred took over the shop while Susan ran the office. But Fred was also going to be away. Susan would have to handle both jobs on her own, and Madge wanted Charlene to help. Charlene didn't mind, because she liked Susan Cole. She was always friendly, and easy to talk to. And working might keep her mind off her problem.

116

*   *   *

"Can you give me a hand with these? asked Susan. She was staggering from the store-room with a load of cartons. Charlene, still in school uniform, had just walked into the hardware shop. She took some of the cartons from Susan, and put them on the counter.

"How's it going? asked Charlene.

"Not bad now," said Susan. "But a couple of hours ago, I was rushed off my feet. Hey, I've just made some coffee. Would you like some?"

They went back into the office which opened from the main store. It was a small room, with old-fashioned equipment — a desk, a filing cabinet, telephone and an aged manual typewriter. In a corner, the coffee percolator was bubbling.

"Sit down," said Susan, pushing aside some dusty books that were on one of the two chairs, "I've got some bikkies somewhere."

She went to the filing cupboard, and found a packet in the spare drawer at the bottom.

"Your favourites, Lennie," said Susan, opening the packet. "Chocolate Ripple."

But right now Charlene didn't feel like eating anything.

"Just coffee," she said, lying. "I had something when I was coming home from school."

"How is school?" asked Susan, as they both

sat drinking coffee together. The door to the shop was wide open, so they could both see if a customer came in.

Charlene shrugged. "So-so," she said. "I can't wait till I finish. Mum wants me to stay on to Matric, but I don't want to."

"Don't rush it," warned Susan, pouring them another coffee. "It's harder to get a job if you haven't got the education."

"How about you?" asked Charlene. She looked around the shabby office with distaste. "You'd hardly call this a career, would you? Working for Mum and Dad."

"I don't mind," said Susan, not taking offence. "It's a good job, and I like your dad. Maybe some day I'll do something better." Charlene noticed she mentioned Fred, and not Madge. That figures, she thought. Her father was an easy-going type, who wouldn't make too many demands as an employer. Anything for a quiet life, that was his philosophy. But Madge, more volatile, could be a difficult person to work with. Demanding and critical of people who didn't live up to her high standards. Charlene knew . . . she'd copped the rough end of Madge's tongue often enough.

Somehow sitting here in the quiet of the back office, Charlene began to feel more relaxed. Once, a customer came in, and Susan went out and served her. It was just for some plastic garbage bags, and she was back in a minute. Charlene thought, not for the first time, how nice it would be to have Susan as a big sister. She was the kind of person one could confide in, calm and always understanding. Henry was okay, but a brother wasn't the same.

It was in this mood that Charlene suddenly broke down and started crying.

Susan, in the middle of telling Charlene how her parents had had to take her out of a private boarding school when she was sixteen (because of the rural recession) was amazed.

"It wasn't that bad," she said, thinking Charlene was upset because her schooling had been cut short. "I didn't mind a bit . . . they were a lot of toffee-nosed snobs there anyway."

Charlene still kept crying.

Susan put an arm around her, unsure what the problem was, but trying to comfort.

"Is anything wrong?" she asked. "Can I help?"

"I hate myself," sobbed Charlene, clinging to her. "I just want to die."

"It can't be anything that terrible," said Susan, still trying to understand. "Whatever it is, you'll find it will all work out."

"No, it won't," said Charlene, and explained her predicament.

"My God," said Susan, aghast. "Are you sure, Lennie?"

"I'm sure," said Charlene, her cheeks wet with tears. "I don't know what to do . . . help me, Susan."

Susan checked the shop for customers, and then closed the door of the office. She would still hear if anyone came in, but right now Charlene was first priority.

"Why don't you tell your mum," she said. "I'm sure she'll understand."

"No, she won't," said Charlene. "If she finds out, she'll kill me."

Knowing Madge, she probably will, Susan thought privately. But she tried to stay calm and encouraging for Charlene's sake. Susan asked who was the father, and Charlene told about the night at the drive-in. But she said she would never let Ian know she ws pregnant. He'd only deny it, anyway. Or he'd lay the blame on someone else. And she'd made it worse by telling her girlfriends nothing had happened that night. If she now turned around and told the opposite story, it would make her look a liar.

Susan said she knew of a girl who had gone interstate, and had her baby at a Catholic home for unwed mothers. The nuns had looked after her and she'd had it adopted. But Charlene didn't fancy that as a solution. She couldn't

120

stand the thought of going through all that pain
and trauma.

"How many periods have you missed?" asked
Susan.

"Two," said Charlene.

"Maybe they'll come back," said Susan, almost as naive in the ways of the body as Charlene. She was the only daughter, youngest of
three, and had had a sheltered upbringing on a
small dairy farm. Her mother had told her only
as much as felt she ought to know — which
amounted to very little. Although Susan was
twenty-two, she had never had a serious relationship with a man. And she was finding it
hard now to give the right advice to Charlene.

"I remember once someone at boarding
school," she said. "She missed a month, although she'd never even been with boy. It was
just a health thing, it happens sometimes. Anyway, she found this old magazine, and it said try
a drink and a hot bath. So she pinched a bit of
the sacrament wine, and then sat in a hot bath.
Sat there for a couple of hours, just turning on
the tap every time it got cold. She nearly
scalded the skin off her body, you should've
seen the red marks all over. But it worked."

"Thanks, Susan," sighed Charlene. "Somehow I think it's going to take more than a hot
bath to get me going again. But thanks anyway."

She finished her coffee, as two customers came into the shop. Susan went in to help one, and Charlene looked after the other. As she weighed some nails, Susan looked anxiously at her employer's daughter. Charlene definitely did look poorly, pale with dark shadows under her eyes. She looked as though she wasn't getting much sleep.

Susan wondered whether she should talk to Fred about it. He seemed an understanding man, and was always approachable. And he'd told her to come with any problems she had. Poor Fred, with all his own problems to cope with . . . that wife of his, who nagged him constantly whenever she came into the office. Susan vowed to herself that if she ever married, she'd never be someone like that. Wives should be caring and compassionate, someone a man enjoyed coming home to. Susan suspected the times Fred had given her a lift home had been to delay going back to Madge.

And now there was Charlene with her terrible secret, unable to turn to anyone.

If only she could help . . .

Chapter 11

CHARLENE had gone home, and Susan was checking on the sales figures, when Fred walked in. He was in a cheerful mood, whistling some tune, as he slapped an order book down on the counter.

"How about that, Susan," he said. "It took me a lot of talking, and a few beers at the pub, but we've got it. The MacInnes account."

'Mac' MacInnes was one of the biggest builders in the shire. An account from him meant a lot of business, Susan smiled, and congratulated Fred.

"That's great, Mr. Mitchell," she said.

Fred winked at Susan, as he put the order book away.

"That's going to mean a bonus for you this Christmas," he said. "And, by the way, don't you think it's time you stopped calling me Mr. Mitchell, and made it Fred?"

Susan thought, not for the first time, what an

attractive man Fred Mitchell was. She remembered the time she'd come to him for a job, straight out of a secretarial course. When her parents had had to withdraw her from boarding school, she'd helped around the farm for a while. Her mother, Merle, was a good cook and housekeeper, and she passed on her skills to her daughter, Susan. It was assumed that one day she'd get married, probably to a farmer. And being able to run a home and raise a family was all that Susan ever aspired to, or felt she needed.

It was her brother Kevin, married with three children, who talked Susan into doing a business course. Kevin, the eldest in the family, worked on the farm and rented a small place nearby. When his father retired, Kevin would take over the property. Kevin urged Susan to learn something that would give her more future than being on a farm all her life. He could see the hardships for women, and had watched their mother battle to keep the farm going . . . growing old before her time. It was Kevin who paid for Susan to learn book-keeping and typing, and then pointed out the ad in the local paper. Madge had placed the advertisement, wanting more time away from the office for her social life. But it was Fred who had interviewed her. He'd been attracted by her naturalness and quiet manner, and had hired her on the spot.

They were still chatting and laughing when Madge arrived . . . her mood as thunderous as Fred's had been cheerful. The wife of the owner of Harrisons had been at the charity meeting, and had made a barbed comment about Mitchell's Hardware not paying its bills on time.

Madge said angrily that she'd brought the account to Fred's attention weeks ago . . . why hadn't he paid it? It was bad enough he was so slack with their personal bills, without letting it interfere with business.

Susan started to intervene, but Madge told her sharply to mind her own business. Ordering Fred to get the cheque for Harrisons in the mail today, she abruptly left.

"I'm sorry, Fred," said Susan. "You told me to take care of the Harrison account, and I just put it to one side and forgot. Why didn't you tell Mrs. Mitchell it was my fault?"

Fred smiled charmingly, and patted Susan on the shoulder.

"No point you getting in Madge's bad books . . . I'm there already," he said. "I reckon I've got broad enough shoulders for both of us. Anyway, don't worry your pretty little head about it. I'll just work back tonight, and bring all the accounts up-to-date. If Madge chooses to spend her time running around to social committees, instead of helping in the shop, you can't be expected to do everything.''

Susan hesitated, then offered to work back with him. She didn't expect to be paid overtime, she told Fred. And besides, she had nothing else to do. All she'd planned was to wash her hair and have an early night at the boarding house where she had a room.

"You're a sweet kid,'' said Fred, patting her again. "I don't know how I'd cope without you.'' Susan glowed under the praise. It was nice to be wanted, even if it was just to catch up on old accounts. And Fred Mitchell was such a nice man, totally unlike that harridan wife of his. She wondered again what had brought them together in the first place. She'd probably trapped Fred into marriage, badgered him into it in a weak moment. She was like that. Susan was sure it couldn't have been love.

Susan started to sort through the accounts file, when Fred stopped her.

"I've got an idea,'' he said, looking at his watch. "Seeing as it's this late, why don't we grab something to eat together? Then we can come back and go on working. Come on, I'll shout you dinner, what d'you say?''

Susan hesitated, wondering whether it might look bad if someone saw them together. This was a small town, and people talked.

As if reading her mind, Fred touched her hand reassuringly.

"Strictly business," he said. "Just a counter tea at the pub, and then we'll come straight back. Look, it'll only take half an hour, and we've got to eat anyway. Where's the harm in it?"

Susan decided she was being silly, and accepted Fred's invitation. She got her coat, and Fred locked up the shop. As he helped her into the car, she felt a strong physical attraction as his face came close to hers. But she dismissed it instantly, knowing he was a married man.

"Okay, Susie, let's go!" said Fred, smiling down at her as he put his foot on the accelerator. And they drove away.

*　　　*　　　*

The half hour grew into an hour, and still they were talking and joking over their meal. Fred had ordered some wine, saying it was a special occasion. Susan didn't normally drink much, but she had several glasses this time, and was feeling very warm and relaxed. She was a very private person, and didn't usually talk much about herself to other people. But she found Fred such a sympathetic and attentive listener, that almost

127

in spite of herself she began to open up.

Susan told Fred about her life with her parents, Merle and Cappy Cole, on the dairy farm a few miles from Coffs Harbour. Her brother Kevin was still working there, but Bob, the second son, had taken off as soon as his High School days were over, saying he didn't intend to spend the rest of his life looking at the back end of cows. He was now part-owner of a pub in another town.

She spoke warmly of her mother, and the way she'd kept the family together, even in hard times. Fred could see Merle Cole was everything Susan aspired to be — warm, caring, conscious of her duties as a wife and mother, and someone who always put her husband and children first.

"She sounds like a nice lady," commented Fred.

"She is," said Susan. "She's a wonderful woman."

It was the perfect opportunity for Fred to talk about his marriage, and he seized it. Fred talked to Susan about his home life, and how empty it had become. He should've married someone like Susan's mother, he told her. Someone who knew how to look after a man. Instead, he found himself saddled with a cold, bad tempered shrew with social ambitions. Fred didn't put it into so many words, but he also implied

128

Madge was frigid.

Susan felt a deep yearning to put her arms around Fred and comfort him. A man like this deserved better than a wife like Madge. He needed a woman who would respect him, who would give him tender, affectionate support when he felt low. He needed to be cared for, loved, cosseted. Without being aware of it, Susan was already seeing herself as that woman.

"I'm sorry," she said. "I wish I could do something, truly."

Fred knew he was treading a very thin line, and had to be careful. Too much too fast, and he could frighten off Susan. He knew she was different from most of the other women he'd made a play for, but it was this difference that attracted him. She was so gentle, so lady-like. He looked on Susan as a challenge.

"Enough of my worries," he said, switching to a joking mood. "I mustn't pull you down into the doldrums, a pretty girl like you should have a smile on her face. Say, did I ever tell you about the time I was selling vacuum cleaners, and this woman asked for a personal demonstration. Then when I got there, I found she lived on the top floor of a five storied block, and the lift wasn't working. And then when I got up there, she'd emptied the bag of the old one all over the carpet, just to make sure I did the job properly. Not only that, but the place looked as though it hadn't been cleaned for a year. And then when I plugged in, the electricity went off . . .''

Susan couldn't help laughing. It broke the tension of all the talk about Fred's marriage.

Back in the dimly-lit office, they worked side by side getting the accounts in order. Susan sorted the overdue ones, and Fred sat writing the cheques. The mellow mood of the dinner was still with them, and Susan was still feeling the effect of the wine.

She glanced at Fred, while he sat writing, and tried to guess his age. He must be forty at least, she thought, although he'd told her he'd married young. But he didn't look it. Madge was probably older than him.

He was an attractive man, with fair hair starting to darken, and a crooked smile that crinkled his eyes. Just the kind of man I want to meet some day, thought Susan. I could share my life with a man like this.

Fred dropped his pen, and they both dived to pick it up, their heads close together. Fred looked at Susan, then took her in his arms and kissed her.

And like Madge twenty years before her, Susan started falling hopelessly in love.

Chapter 12

MADGE could see Charlene was desperately worried about something. As Madge sat in the living room after dinner, darning Henry's socks, she watched Charlene sprawled listlessly in an armchair.

Usually at this time of day, Charlene was on the phone talking nonstop to one of her friends. It was a source of irritation to Madge, those endless calls just after Charlene got home from school.

"What've you got to talk about, when you've just been all day with Cynthia (or Helen or Jill)," she demanded. "Those calls aren't free, y'know. If you had to pay the bills around here, you'd think twice about making them. Anyone would think money grows on trees."

But Charlene hadn't been making any calls for weeks now. She'd even stopped watching television. All she seemed to do now was moon about the house looking listless.

Perhaps I am too hard on her, Madge thought. After all, she's nearly sixteen. She hasn't asked to go out since that night I put my foot down about the drive-in, and locked her in her room. Maybe she's still moping about that boy she mentioned. Madge remembered back to her own teenage years, and knew how much puppy love could hurt.

She put down the half-darned sock, and decided to make an attempt to get through to her daughter.

"How is that new boy you mentioned . . . Alec, or was it Ian?"

Charlene stiffened at the mention of the name.

"Ian," she said. "What about him?"

"I thought you might like to ask him some night for dinner," said Madge. "You know I always like to meet the friends you go around with. I could cook a nice pot-roast, and make a lemon meringue pie. Boys always like lemon meringue."

"No, thanks," said Charlene curtly.

Normally Madge would lose her temper at Charlene's rebuff, but because she felt something was troubling Charlene, she persevered with her overtures.

"I hope you're not still holding a grudge against me for that night I wouldn't let you go

132

out," she said. "You know I've only got your best interests at heart. Anything I do, it's for your own good."

Still Charlene didn't respond.

Madge was starting to get worried. Although she and Charlene had plenty of battles, it wasn't like Charlene to stay mad for so long. Usually she just blew up, said what she thought, and then forgot about it next day. But this mood of Charlene's had dragged on now for weeks.

Madge tried another tack.

"Charlene, is there something worrying you?" she asked gently. "Because if there is, I want to help you. I know we've had our differences in the past, but I am your mother. There can't be anything bad enough that you can't share it with me. Is it something at school? Are you worried about your exams?"

Charlene's eyes filled with tears, as she looked at Madge. She knew that in spite of everything, Madge was genuinely trying to help. And this might be the moment to tell the truth. The most Madge could do was yell at her. And it would be a relief to finally get the whole thing out in the open.

Charlene was about to confess, when Henry bowled in the door.

"Hi, everyone," he said. "Any food left over?"

Madge's concern immediately switched to Henry. Forgetting all about the problem of Charlene, she was on her feet.

"I kept your dinner warm for you in the oven," she said. "When you didn't come home, I put some on a plate."

Henry put his arms around Madge and kissed her.

"Sorry, Mum," he said. "I should've rung. But I was having a game of snooker and kind of forgot the time. Thanks for keeping my dinner . . . you're an angel."

Madge pushed him away in pretend exasperation, but she was smiling.

The two went through to the kitchen, leaving Charlene on her own.

Typical, she thought, her unhappiness now giving way to exasperation. All Henry has to do is breeze through the door, and my problems are forgotten. And Madge didn't even tell him off for being late. Now if I'd waltzed in a couple of hours after mealtime . . .

In the kitchen, Madge was listening to Henry tell of another fruitless search for a job. She knew jobs were hard to find for young people, but she also wasn't sure how hard Henry was trying to get one. Too bad that one with Ace Manufacturing had fallen through, and all because of Fred. If he hadn't bought that cheap lot of paint, and then made things worse when he wouldn't give a refund. It was typical of Fred, always trying to do a bit of a fiddle. But so far as Madge was concerned, it had cost Henry his job.

"By the way, I'm not going to be home to-night," she told Henry. "There's a church social, Beryl's picking me up in half an hour."

"Suits me," grinned Henry, as he mopped up the gravy. "I'm going to be out myself."

He'd hoped to meet Linda, so they could talk over plans for the ball. But Linda had begged off, saying she had a migraine. So he was going out with Jacko and the gang instead.

That ball. The thought of it was beginning to worry Henry. He had a feeling Linda was losing interest, and he knew this was his one big chance to consolidate the relationship. If he could impress her, play the big spender, and make it a night to remember, then he was fairly sure that Linda would be his. But if she once suspected he had no money . . . Henry shuddered. The thought was too horrible to contemplate. Somehow or other, he had to get to that ball.

"Don't suppose you could lend me a few dollars?" he asked Madge.

"And waste it on those drunken louts you call your friends?" Madge responded. "Not on your life. I've got better things to do with it."

135

Henry sighed. Sometimes Madge could be very difficult. And lately she seemed to be getting even more tense and touchy. It can't be Dad, Henry thought. He hardly ever seems to be around these days, and when he is, they're barely speaking. Maybe she's approaching that time of life.

As Madge got ready to go to the social, she wondered where Fred was — and what he was doing tonight. He hadn't been home for dinner for ages. And when he did come home late at night, all he did was fall into bed.

She wondered if there was another woman. After the incident of the letter, she knew Fred would be very careful to hide any more evidence. He could be very clever at covering up, he'd done it in the past. Madge sniffed his clothing, trying to detect the whiff of perfume. But so far, nothing. Just the smell of cigarettes and stale beer.

Madge knew from all the old warning signals. When Fred was home now, he seemed unusually cheerful. He had given Charlene ten dollars to spend on herself, and was even making an effort to get along with Henry. He hadn't even been angered when she accidentally threw out his favourite cardigan in the clothing collection, saying cardigans were for old men anyway. Then soon after, he went and bought a whole lot of new clothing, going to the trendy shop where Henry shopped rather than the department store where they had a family account.

Fred had also had his hairstyle changed, going in for a layered look. Personally, Madge didn't like it, and told him. She much preferred the old short back and sides. But Fred's argument was that he was a well-known businessman. He had to look good, and move with the times.

Madge was still thinking about Fred's new hairdo, as Beryl sounded her car horn and she started to go outside. At the door, she suddenly remembered the conversation with Charlene.

"Was there something you wanted to talk to me about?" she asked, her hand already on the doorknob.

Charlene looked up from the book she was reading.

"Forget it," she said.

Madge promptly forgot it. She warned Charlene to make sure she did her homework, after she'd tidied the kitchen and done the dishes. And then she was gone.

*   *   *

Jacko and his mates were lounging outside the pinball parlour, when Henry joined them.

They were talking about the warehouse job, with Jacko all for pulling it off.

"Come on, Henry," urged Dakka. "Be in it."

But Henry still hesitated. He was all for something that had a bit of adventure and excitement, and had always gone along with anything Jacko suggested before. But this was the big one. They'd never gone as far as robbing a warehouse. Henry knew if he joined in and got caught, he could finish up in jail. And spending the next few years of his life behind bars wasn't something that particularly appealed to him. Not when he was having such a good time.

"Count me out," said Henry. "You guys go ahead if you want to."

Jacko didn't mind Henry not joining in. It would be one less to share the proceeds. But he needed a car for the job, and Henry was the fastest at hot-wiring. So he applied some pressure.

"How's that new girl of yours, Henry?" he asked off-handedly. "The one we met up at Dino's."

"Linda? She's fine," replied Henry. "Everything's sweet."

Jacko turned the screws a bit.

"Hear she only likes guys who've got money," he said. "Bit out of her class, aren't you?"

Henry knew he was being needled, but his pride came before his commonsense.

"Okay, Jacko," he said. "So what's the deal?"

Jacko explained that Henry didn't have to be involved with the warehouse robbery, if he didn't want to. Just so long as he kept quiet. But if he would hot-wire a car for them to use, a wagon or something with a large boot, they'd cut him in for a hundred bucks. Henry hesitated a moment, and agreed.

Alone in the house, Charlene took a bottle of gin from her schoolbag. She'd used the money Fred gave her, and asked Big Al to get her brother to buy it for her. Big Al had hidden it in her locker, then slipped it to her in a brown paper bag, before school. When she'd wanted to know why Charlene bought it, Charlene had said she was going to a party with some of Henry's friends.

Charlene wrinkled her nose in distaste, as she took the top off and sniffed it. She'd tried everything else in the past week, even a dose of castor oil. Now it was the old hot bath and bottle of gin trick. Charlene tried to be flippant with herself, but as she poured the gin she noticed her hand was shaking. What if it didn't work? She drank the gin quickly, trying not to think, and poured another. Outwardly she seemed calm. But somewhere inside was a desperately anxious and scared little girl.

In town, Henry watched as his three friends drove off in the car he'd just hot-wired. It was a blue sedan, four doors, with a roomy boot. Jacko figured they could stack enough in it to make the job worthwhile. As they drove off, he called back a jeering remark about Henry not having the guts to go after the real dough. Henry stood there, a tight knot in his stomach. he wasn't worried about them thinking him chicken. But he was still concerned that he'd let himself be talked into the deal.

As Henry walked away to go back home, he made up his mind. Never again . . . no more hot-wiring cars, no more joyrides. Maybe it was time he grew up a little.

Back at the Mitchell house, Charlene was in a hot bath and feeling woozy. She'd drunk half the bottle, and the room was beginning to spin around her. She started feeling sick, but put it down to her pregnancy. Charlene looked down at her body, trying to imagine what it would look like if this didn't work. She'd have to leave school, of course. And Madge would probably insist she left town as well. Maybe she'd send her down to stay with her Uncle Max in Erinsborough. One thing Charlene was sure about, and that was Madge wouldn't want a pregnant daughter hanging around Coffs Harbour. The shame of it would just about kill Madge . . . having people gossip, whispers behind closed doors. Madge had always been very conscious of her position in the community, and fancied herself as a social leader. Thinking about her mother made Charlene reach for the bottle of gin again. As the fiery liquid burned down her throat, Charlene felt the room swimming around her again.

She suddenly realised she could pass out, lying there in the hot bath. And if she slipped under the water, she would drown. Charlene clung to the edge of the bath, desperately trying to remain conscious. Then feeling she was going to vomit, she tried to climb out.

As she stood there, unsteady on her feet, things started to blur. She could see her blue dressing-gown on its hook behind the bathroom door. Closer, draped over a stool, was a bath towel. Charlene started to get out, then fell heavily. She felt her stomach hit the edge of the bath, and she sprawled headfirst on the wet floor tiles. Pain swept over her. Then she passed out.

Chapter 13

H ENRY unlocked the front door, and walked in. He called out for Charlene, but there was no answer.

Henry grinned to himself. So she'd slipped out, knowing Madge wasn't home to keep an eye on her. Good old Lennie . . . when the cat's away, the mice will play. He only hoped she'd get home before Madge came back from her church social, or there'd be hell to pay.

Henry headed for the bathroom, to go to the toilet. When he opened the door, he was stunned by what he saw — Charlene naked and unconscious, lying in a pool of blood.

Henry's stomach was a weak one at the best of times, and he felt sick. Then he pulled himself together, his only thought to help Charlene. Covering her with the dressing-gown, he carried her in his arms to her bedroom.

As Henry sat beside the bed, holding Lennie's hand, she started to groan and stir. Then,

142

through the mists of alcohol and pain, she began to regain consciousness.

"You idiot," said Henry. "What the hell d'you think you're trying to do to yourself?" But his voice was gentle.

Charlene knew she couldn't hide the truth from him any more. And she didn't want to.

"I'm pregnant," she said.

Henry was even more gentle, as he looked down at the tiny, white-faced figure in the bed.

"Not any more you're not," he said. "I think we should call a doctor."

Charlene clung to him, and begged him not to.

"If you get a doctor, Mum'll find out," she said.

"Please, Henry . . . you've got to keep this a secret."

Tenderness for his sister suddenly over-whelmed Henry, and he felt tears in his eyes, as he held Charlene close to him . . . asking her why she hadn't confided in him, let him help? He told her again she was an idiot, for believing an old wives' tale like that. Didn't she realise how dangerous it was . . . didn't she realise she could have killed herself?

"I know, I know," said Charlene. "I just couldn't think straight. I'm sorry."

Henry told her it was lucky he was the one who walked in when he did. What if it had been one of their parents who'd come home and gone into the bathroom?

Mention of the bathroom reminded Henry that there was some cleaning up to do. Charlene wanted to help, but he insisted she stay in bed. He even got her a hot water bottle, and made her a warm chocolate drink. Then he rolled up his sleeves, and went to work.

Charlene lay back and closed her eyes. Her head had started to throb, probably from all the gin she'd drunk. And her body ached all over. But she was calmer now, knowing Henry was out there looking after everything.

Dear Henry. He might have his faults, but she loved him more than anyone else in the world.

When he'd scrubbed the bathroom, Henry spent the rest of the evening sitting with Charlene, holding her hand, and trying to comfort her. She was still very weepy, but the pain was beginning to go. Across her stomach a blue bruise was starting to form, a reminder of what had happened in the bathroom. She had a piece of sticking plaster on her forehead, where it had hit the slippery tiles.

Henry was still holding her hand, and talking to her, when they heard Madge let herself in the front door.

Charlene, agitated, clung to Henry again in panic.

"Don't tell Mum," she said. "Promise me you won't tell."

Henry promised, and left, turning off the light as he went. In the kitchen he found Madge grimly looking at the dirty dishes.

"That Charlene!" Madge was saying. "Never does a thing I tell her, it really gets my goat. Couldn't you have cleaned up the kitchen, Henry? Most of it is your mess anyway."

Henry told Madge he'd only just that minute arrived home.

When Madge looked as though she was heading for Charlene's room, on the warpath, Henry intercepted her . . . flashing his most winning smile.

"She's asleep," he said. "The place was in darkness when I came in. Why don't you wait till tomorrow? Come on, sit down, and I'll make you a nice cup of tea."

Madge said she'd already had one, but she allowed herself to be led to the living room. Then as Henry settled her into an armchair, and massaged the back of her neck, she sighed as she felt some of the tension leaving her. She put a hand up and touched him.

"You're a good son," she said. "I don't know what I'd do without you. At least you worry about how I feel . . . not like Charlene. All she cares about is herself."

145

If you only knew, thought Henry, gently kneading Madge's neck and shoulders with his fingers. Lennie could have died tonight, caring about you . . . caring what you thought, and how you'd feel about having a pregnant daughter.

Aloud, he said mildly that Madge shouldn't be so hard on Charlene. Madge, relaxing under Henry's touch, admitted she was harsh sometimes . . . "but it's for her own good," she added.

"I worry about her," she told Henry. "I know all the things that can happen to a young girl. Charlene should count herself lucky that she's got a mother to protect her."

And in the darkness of her room, Charlene cried herself to sleep.

Chapter 14

BREAKFAST at the Mitchell house was never the brightest of meals, but next morning hit an all time low. Fred, suffering from a hangover after his night out with Susan, was short and snappy. Henry was unusually quiet and preoccupied, still thinking of last night. And Madge had burnt the toast.

She decided not to waste it, and scraped the charred sides into the tidy bin. Fred looked at it with distaste, as Madge handed him his plate of bacon and eggs.

"We in mourning or something?" he asked, eyeing the blackened piece of bread. Madge, who always prided herself on her cooking, was quick to take offence.

"Next time, make it yourself," she snapped, as she went back to frying some more bacon. Fred got up and made a production of tipping the toast into the bin, and then putting some more in the toaster. Madge gave him a dirty look, and was about to say something when Charlene came into the room.

Charlene hadn't had much sleep, and looked pale and ill. She'd dragged herself out of bed to go to school, not wanting to draw attention to herself, but the sight of Madge frying bacon turned her stomach over. It wasn't the morning sickness, she was over that now. But she was suffering from the effects of drinking so much gin.

"Good lord, Charlene, you look like death warmed up," said Madge, immediately concerned. "I knew you were sickening or something. You've probably got this virus that's going around, Beryl told me she was in bed two weeks with it. Now go straight back to bed, and I'll ring the school."

For once Charlene didn't want to argue with Madge, and listlessly agreed. She exchanged a glance with Henry as she went back to her room.

Madge put the bacon she'd been cooking for Charlene on to Henry's plate, and sat down to have her own breakfast. Fred was still eating silently, looking moody. His mind was on Susan, and their next date together. She was still feeling guilt pangs about going out with a married man, but he'd managed to convince her that Madge didn't care. She could see it for herself, anyway. Every time Madge came into the shop, all she did was find fault with the way Fred was running it.

Fred knew he had to handle this new love affair very carefully. One wrong move, and he could blow it. Susan wasn't like all the others, which was part of her appeal. Fred was pretty certain she was still a virgin, which was unusual these days. But he also knew she was the kind of girl who wouldn't go to bed with a man unless she loved him.

Fred knew Susan was falling for him, he was sure of that. He could tell by the look in her eyes, the way she responded to his kisses. All he had to do was sit tight and play a waiting game. Choose the right place, and the right moment.

Aloud he said: "Don't keep dinner for me tonight. We've run into a few problems with some of the old stock. Susan's agreed to stay back and work with me."

"You work that girl too hard," said Madge. "Just because she's willing, you take advantage. Why don't you get Henry to give you a hand?"

Henry cut in quickly, and said he was seeing Linda. Fred told Madge that Susan didn't mind the work, besides he'd be paying her overtime. And she was the one who had offered.

"I still think you overwork her," said Madge. "Beryl said she saw the lights on the other

149

night, when she was going past . . . must've
been six thirty or seven. The girl's entitled to a
life of her own. Just show a little consider-
ation.''

Madge wondered, not for the first time, what
kind of life Susan led when she wasn't working
in the office. She knew she roomed at a board-
ing-house, and had a family somewhere in the
country. Beyond that, she knew very little
about the office worker Fred had hired a year or
so ago. Madge supposed she had a boyfriend,
but if she did, she didn't talk about him. One of
those quiet types, who kept to herself. But she
was efficient at her job, and Charlene and
Henry both liked her.

Madge had been a bit surprised at the time by
Fred's choice of an office secretary. Knowing
his taste in females, she thought he'd go for
someone more flamboyant and tarty. Maybe
Fred had some sense, after all. The flashy types
weren't always the good workers. And Susan
was honest and conscientious, anxious to please
her employers. Yes, we could have done worse,
thought Madge with some satisfaction. After all
the years she'd slaved to build up the business,
Susan was a godsend.

Madge was about to pour some more coffee,
when there was a knock at the front door.
When she answered it, she found two policemen

standing there. One she recognised as Dawson, from the time before when he'd come around. He asked for Henry.

Madge's heart sank. Surely Henry hadn't been joyriding again? She'd had a good long talk with him after the last incident, and he'd promised faithfully to turn over a new leaf. And meeting this girl Linda had been good for him. For the first time he seemed to be making a serious effort to find a job. Madge had been breathing easy, feeling Henry had probably sown all his wild oats and was now going to settle down to some responsibility. Now all her old fears came back again . . .

In the kitchen, Henry overheard and turned pale. He knew there was nothing he could do, except sit tight and hope his mother could bluff it out. What had brought the police around to his place? Had they found out he'd hot-wired a car last night. It had been a deserted back street, and he could have sworn no one had seen him. But maybe someone had.

Fred was now at the front door, peering over Madge's shoulder and blundering into the conversation. He recognised one of the cops by sight, Mick Jones. He'd once delivered a load of timber to his house.

"What's going on here?" he asked, as Madge blocked the door like a tigress defending her young.

151

"G'day, Fred," said Jones. "Is young Henry at home? We'd just like a word with him."

"What about?" asked Fred. He liked to keep on the right side of the police, just as a kind of insurance policy. But he was also wary where the law was concerned. No sense saying too much, until he knew the full story.

"Just a couple of routine questions," said Dawson. "Would you mind telling me who was home here last night?"

Madge and Fred both said they were out. When asked about Henry, Fred said his son had told him he was going out with his mates. They looked at Madge to confirm it. She started to feel nervous, not sure of saying the right thing.

"He was here when I got home," she said.

Dawson asked what time that was. Madge said around eleven.

"We'd still like to talk to him," said the other.

Henry knew he couldn't put it off any longer, and joined his parents at the front door. Madge explained the situation.

"That's right," said Henry, flashing a disarming smile. "I was home around eight thirty."

Madge felt her stomach settle in a tight knot. Why was Henry lying? He had told her he just got in when she'd arrived.

Madge turned to the police . . . was this about joyriding? The police played it cagey, saying it was something like that.

Madge looked at Henry, and came to a decision. She'd always protected him before, but it couldn't go on forever. Much as she loved her only son, Madge's commonsense told her Henry had a weakness for easy money and the good life . . . And if she didn't knock that weakness on the head right here and now, he would never amount to anything.

"I'm sorry, Henry," she said. "I'm not going to help you."

She faced the two policemen.

"He told me he got home just before I did," she said to them.

As they took Henry off, to talk to him at the station, he looked back at her. For one terrible moment, Madge wondered if she'd done the right thing. Henry's look said she'd betrayed him. It was the look of a small boy, let down by the person he loved and trusted. Madge wanted to go to him, take him in her arms and comfort him. Instead she had to stand and watch him led away.

"Well, you really did it this time," commented Fred drily, as Henry went off in the police car. "I've got to hand it to you, Madge, I never thought you'd have the guts."

Madge didn't answer, still feeling devastated. Would Henry ever forgive her? Could she make

153

him understand she was doing it to help him?

"Not that the young lout doesn't deserve it," added Fred. "He's had it coming for a long time . . . all those no good hooligans he hangs around with. I hope when he gets to the station, they throw the book at him."

Madge jerked herself back to what Fred was saying.

"Henry will be all right," she said confidently. "I made some inquiries, last time it happened. It's not as though he was stealing or anything. All they'll do for a joyride will be put him on a good behaviour bond. Maybe it will make him see some sense, and realise the kind of company he's keeping."

Back in the kitchen, Madge had lost her appetite. She tipped the remains of her breakfast in the tidy, and sat thinking, as Fred went off to work.

That look Henry had given her as he went off . . . it hurt. It was the only time in her life she'd ever let him down. But she had to be strong, for Henry's sake. It was for his own good. And after all, it wasn't as if he'd go to jail . . .

Chapter 15

A T the police station, Henry was taken into a room and fingerprinted. The room was a bare one, sparsely furnished with a table, chairs, and a filing cabinet in one corner. Overhead was one single electric light.

Henry started thinking about all the movies he'd seen, when the suspect sat in a chair under a glaring spotlight, and was put through the third degree. But it was nothing like that. After the fingerprinting, two detectives came in and introduced themselves as Harvey and Phillips. Then they started to question him . . . quietly at first, then with increasing toughness.

Henry said he missed seeing his mates, so he went home. Detective Phillips pointed out that Henry had told his mother he arrived home just before her, at eleven o'clock. Henry said that was only an excuse for not having done the dishes. He'd been home for hours . . . his sister will verify it.

Detective Harvey asked what he did at home. Henry said he watched television. What programs? Henry hesitated . . . he couldn't remember offhand, it wasn't anything great.

The detectives exchanged looks. They told him a warehouse had been robbed last night, and the guard bashed. He was now in hospital, with severe head injuries. But before he was bashed, he'd recognised one of the gang as Darryl Andrews. He'd gone to school with one of his kids, and the guard swore he'd know him anywhere. Nasty bit of work, always getting into trouble. He couldn't identify the others, and didn't know his attacker, because he'd been hit from behind. All he could say was that there were at least three of them.

"So what's this got to do with me?" asked Henry, trying to play it very cool. Inwardly, he could feel trouble coming. Had someone seen him hot-wire that car? Where were the others, and what were they doing? If the cops had dragged him along to the station to try and get information, they had another thing coming. There was no way he'd dob in his best mates.

But he was feeling glad he'd not allowed himself to be talked into the warehouse job by Jacko. Pinching videos was one thing, bashing someone was another. There's no way Henry would have been involved in something like that, violence was against his nature. Going home early when he did had been a wise decision, in more ways than one.

Henry made up his mind that no matter how much they pressured him, he wouldn't let on he'd known about the warehouse robbery. All he had to do was sit tight and play dumb. He knew nothing. Unless he'd been spotted with the car, he was in the clear.

Phillips continued to question, telling Henry they knew Dakka was one of the gang Henry knocked around with. How about the others, Peter Nesbit and Kevin Jackson? How many of them had been in the warehouse job? Henry denied knowing anything about it . . . covering for his mates as well. If the guard reckoned he'd seen Dakka, he must have been mistaken. He'd never heard any of them talking about pulling a stunt like that. It must have been someone else.

As Phillips put on the pressure, and Henry continued to deny any knowledge, a police-woman came into the room and talked in an undertone to Detective Harvey. She left, and Harvey walked over to the table where Henry was sitting.

"So you still claim you know nothing about it?" he asked.

Henry stuck to his story. He knew nothing, and he'd been home all night.

The detective looked grim. He explained a car had been found abandoned that morning, and had been identified as the same one which was spotted by the security guard at the site of the warehouse robbery. The car had been carefully cleaned of prints — except under the dashboard, where it had been hot-wired. The fingerprints matched Henry's.

"Now would you like to think again about where you were last night?" said Harvey. "And this time, we want the truth, sonny boy."

Henry blanched. There was no way he could bluff his way out of this one. He was in big trouble.

*   *   *

At home, Madge went about her housework, worrying about Henry. Had she made a mistake by putting him in . . . should she have covered for him again? She still couldn't forget that look on his face, when they took him away. Then she decided she'd done the right thing . . . he had to learn. She hated the thought of him being put on a good behaviour bond, but it may make him take another look at life. She had done what was best for him.

Charlene came out from her room, looking wan.

"I thought I told you to stay in bed," said Madge, concerned at how ill her daughter looked. She'd never seen Charlene quite this bad before, so pale and drawn. It was obvious she was coming down with something.

"I'm okay," said Charlene. "Just got sick of staying in bed, that's all." She looked around the room. "Where's Henry?"

Madge hesitated, knowing how fond Charlene was of her brother. Then she decided the best thing was to tell the truth about what happened that morning. After all, Charlene was bound to find out sooner or later.

Charlene was shocked, as Madge explained the visit from the police. She had gone straight to sleep, shutting her bedroom door, and hadn't heard the commotion.

When Madge told how she'd refused to lie again for Henry, and give him an alibi, Charlene became even more upset. How could her mother let the police take him? He couldn't have done anything wrong last night, he was there with her from early evening.

"I know how much you think of Henry," said Madge "and I appreciate you're only trying to help him. But two wrongs don't make a right. Henry told me himself that when he got home, you were sleeping. He said all the lights were out. Now it's bad enough that I've covered for

159

Henry in the past. I won't have you lying for him as well."

*   *   *

At the police station, Henry was still in the interview room being interrogated. But he was no longer cool and confident. He was now fighting for his freedom.

Time and time again they put him through his original story, trying to get him to admit to the robbery. They told him it would go better for him to face up to it and tell the truth. Lying would only go against him in the long run. It was obvious he rigged the car, and it had been used for the robbery. Who was driving the car? How many others had been in on it with him? Where were the goods now?

Henry knew his only defence would be to say as little as possible. He was determined not to put his mates in, and hoped like hell they were laying low somewhere. He remembered Pete's family had a weekend shack out in the bush. Maybe they'd all gone there.

"Look, Mitchell," said Harvey, starting for the first time to lose his temper. "We know you fixed that car, your prints are all over it. And we know you were with your mates in town last

160

night. So why don't you stop mucking us around, and tell the truth. It'll go easier for you in the long run.''

But still Henry refused to admit anything. They were still talking, as Jacko and Dakka came in. The two were in handcuffs, escorted by a uniformed policeman. Jacko gave Henry a look as he saw him with the detective. Henry wasn't sure what the look meant . . . surely Jacko didn't think he was pulling the plug on them?

*   *   *

At home, Charlene was still trying to defend Henry. But when Madge wanted to know what they were doing all evening, Charlene was forced into silence. How could she tell her mother that Henry had spent the whole time cleaning out the bathroom, and caring for her after the miscarriage? Madge read the silence as guilt, for covering up for Henry. She softened a little, saying she knew how upset Charlene must be feeling about her brother. Didn't Charlene realise how bad Madge was feeling herself?

Sometimes a parent had to be cruel, to be kind. Henry had got into bad company, and bad ways, and if he wasn't pulled up now Heaven knows what might happen to him.

When he got home, she'd make it up to him. She'd explain why she did it . . . In time, Henry would understand.

Charlene didn't see it Madge's way. She was scathing in her criticism of her mother, saying that as Henry was her favourite the least she could do was stand by him.

"How can you say things like that?" said Madge, deeply offended. "You know I love both of you. It's just that you'll never let me get close enough to you to show it."

She put her arms around Charlene, hugging her, repeating again that she loved both of them. To Madge's surprise, Charlene started to weep and cling to her. She hadn't done that since she was a small child.

The moment was broken by the phone ringing. It was Henry from the station, he told his mother he was allowed one call. As Madge listened, she could hardly believe what he was telling her.

Madge put down the phone, looking stunned. Charlene asked what was wrong.

"It's your brother," said Madge.

"Are they charging him with joyriding?" asked Charlene.

Madge looked at Charlene, agony showing on her face.

"It's worse than that," she said. "Much, much worse."

162

Chapter 16

A T the shop, Fred was telling a sympathetic Susan how Henry had been hauled off by the police. And of course, like Fred, Madge had blamed him.

Fred's opinion was that a few hours down at the police station would do no harm to Henry. It might help pull him together, and give him a bit of backbone. Half his problems had been caused by Madge spoiling him . . . she'd shut her eyes to all his faults, ever since he was knee high to a grasshopper. Fred said he'd done his best to instil some discipline, but he was undermined at every turn by Madge. Henry only had to smile at her, and she gave in to everything he wanted. No wonder the boy was now in trouble.

Susan, concerned, took his hand.

"Perhaps you should be down there with him." she said.

Again, Fred lied.

"I tried, but he didn't want me," he said. "All

he wants is to hide behind his mother's skirts. He knows he can get around her. Honestly, sometimes I feel like taking off and never coming back. No one would miss me, that's for sure.''

Susan said she was sure Charlene would. Fred shrugged. Maybe, maybe not. She'd been a bit moody lately. All wrapped up in her teenage world, she'd hardly notice if he were there or not.

Mention of Charlene reminded Susan of their talk the other day. She hoped Charlene was all right. Maybe she'd made a mistake about the pregnancy. Worry and guilt could bring on symptoms, Susan had heard that. She made a mental note to check with Charlene again, next time she saw her. If she really were pregnant, she'd try to persuade her to go and see a doctor.

There was a phone call from a customer, wanting to check on an unpaid account. Susan answered it, handling the inquiry in her usual businesslike, charming manner. Fred watched her as she talked, noticing again the warm, inviting curve of her lips, the way her hair curled in tendrils around the nape of her neck.

"Leave it off the hook," he said. "I want to talk to you."

Susan put it down, and looked at Fred.

"I just want to say, I don't know how I'd cope

164

without you," he said. "My life's a mess . . . you're the only one who really understands me."

Love for the man rushed over Susan, and overwhelmed her. She knew it was wrong, but she couldn't help herself. Fred only had to touch her, and she turned to jelly. If only he weren't married . . . if only he were free and single. She wanted to comfort and care for him, give him all the loving support he didn't get from his family.

That Madge Mitchell, she thought, so cold and unresponsive to a man's needs. Fred hadn't talked to her directly about his sex life, he was too much of a gentleman for that. But she could read between the lines.

Madge was one of those women who took everything and gave nothing. Susan knew that kind. Social position was the only thing she wanted out of marriage. That and a breadwinner. Fred had told her of the long hours he'd worked to set up the business, trying to give Madge everything she wanted. He'd worked his guts out.

But nothing satisfied Madge. The more he spent, the more she asked for. And she gave nothing back in return — no love, no warmth. Not even the physical comfort to which a man was entitled. Susan was pretty sure the marriage had been one in name only for a number of years now. Fred was too decent to put it in so many words, but she could tell.

Fred took the account she was holding in her hand, put it down and pulled her to him. He kissed her gently at first, then with increasing passion. And Susan responded. This man was more wonderful than anyone she had ever met before. He brought out the depths of passion she never knew she had. It was wrong, she knew. But she couldn't help herself.

*   *   *

At the police station, a frightened Henry was still insisting he knew nothing about the hot-wired car. He had no idea how his fingerprints were on it. And he had nothing to do with the warehouse robbery or the bashing of the guard.

But Henry now knew that his mates had put him on. They'd lied, trying to save their own skins by appearing cooperative. So much for loyalty. He'd risked his skin to protect and help them, and now all three had turned on him.

Jacko and Dakka had claimed Henry was with them. They'd also told the cops he was the one who bashed the guard. The guard had been hit from behind, and hadn't seen his attacker. But he knew there was a third boy. Both Jacko and Dakka had signed a statement that the third one was Henry. Henry now knew that it must have been the still missing Pete.

Madge arrived, with a solicitor. Tearful, she flung her arms around Henry, but he didn't respond. the solicitor told Madge she had the right to be present during the interview, but Henry said he didn't want her. He preferred to be on his own.

In a small interview room, Henry told the solicitor the story. Yes, he had hot-wired the car. But that was the only thing he'd lied to the police about. He'd gone home immediately afterwards, and spent the evening with his sister. The solicitor, making notes, said it was a pity Henry hadn't told the truth in the first place. Now that he'd been caught out in one lie, it was going to be that much harder to convince anyone he hadn't been near the warehouse.

Henry looked pleadingly at the solicitor.

"You do believe me, don't you?" he asked.

"Whether I believe you or not has nothing to do with it," said the solicitor crisply. "My job's to defend you, and try to get you off."

Madge, waiting outside and sick with worry, decided to ring Fred and tell him what was happening. After all, they were both his parents. Henry had turned his back on her, but he might be prepared to talk to Fred. Whatever their differences, they were still father and son. And Madge also felt a desperate need for some comfort herself. She had no one else to turn to.

A police officer directed her to a pay phone, and she put in the coins. She knew Fred would be at the shop, he'd told her he'd be working there all day. But when she dialled, all she got was an engaged signal.

Madge tried twice again, and then put a call in to Charlene. She asked Charlene to keep ringing, and tell her father where Madge was. Charlene asked how everything was going. Madge said she didn't know, but she was hoping for the best.

The best . . . mused Madge, as she put the phone down. What did that mean? All her world seemed to be crumbling around her. Charlene was as difficult and temperamental as ever and — apart from that brief moment this morning — determined to keep her mother at a distance. Henry was still angry with her for what she'd done. For the first time in many years, Madge had to admit to herself that she needed Fred. She needed someone to lean on, someone to share her worry. If only he were here . . .

Fred was the first one to break off from the passionate clinch, saying he was sorry . . . it wasn't fair to involve Susan in all his personal

168

problems. But she was so sweet, so understanding, that he couldn't help himself. It had been a long time since anyone had showed him any affection.

Susan told him not to blame himself, she knew he wouldn't do anything to hurt her. Besides, she was an adult, able to make up her own mind on things.

Again, Fred talked about leaving, saying that maybe he'd go on the road again. Travel north, try and find some peace and happiness. No one around the place would miss him anyway.

Susan went very quiet, then she said she'd miss him. Fred appeared touched. He told her he shouldn't say it, but he couldn't help himself . . . he was in love with her. She'd come to represent all the warmth and loving that he missed at home.

"I love you too," said Susan.

Fred kissed her, saying again and again how he couldn't believe it. He was the luckiest man in the world. But he desperately needed to hold her even closer, somewhere away from prying eyes. Just the two of them. There was this small motel a few kilometres out of town . . . Susan hesitated, not sure whether she wanted to take this next step. She loved Fred, but all her upbringing was sending off alarm bells. A customer came into the shop, and was banging on the counter for attention. Fred, annoyed that the romantic mood had been broken, went out to serve. Susan put the phone back on the hook. As soon as she did, it started ringing. At the other end, an impatient Charlene was wondering why it had taken so long to get through. She told Susan she needed to talk to her father urgently.

Fred came back, and Susan handed him the receiver.

"Anything wrong?" she asked, when Fred hung up.

"It's Henry," said Fred. "The young hooligan's got himself into real trouble. Now he's been arrested for a bashing and robbery . . . I knew it would come to this one day."

"D'you want to go to him?" asked Susan. "I can mind the shop if you do."

Fred knew this could be the turning point in their relationship. He was well aware that Susan was head over heels in love with him, and he was more than fond of her himself. Part of it was physical attraction, but part of it was also male ego. It pleased and flattered him to think that in his forties, approaching middle age, he could still win a younger woman. It gave him back his confidence.

Fred was almost certain that if the customer hadn't come into the shop, he could have persuaded Susan to go to the motel with him. She was already on the edge, hesitating. All it needed was a little push.

Fred gave it that push, turning on the best acting performance of his life. He played the part of a broken man, saying Charlene had told him Madge and Henry didn't need him. Madge had said she could handle it all herself. Now things at home would be even worse, with Madge on his back every minute. She'd blame him for Henry's mess, as she always did. Henry, as usual, would take his mother's side.

Fred broke down, choked with emotion. "I'm no good to anyone," he said. "Even you don't want me."

Susan didn't hesitate any longer. She went to Fred, and cradled him lovingly in her arms.

"I do, I do," she said, softly. "I love you, I want to be with you. Let's go to that motel at lunchtime."

As Fred made a pretence of pulling himself together, he turned his head away and smiled. For once Henry had done him a good turn.

*   *   *

At the police station, Madge still waited. She looked at her watch, noticing it was almost one o'clock. The solicitor had gone, and Henry was in a holding cell. And still no sign of Fred.

171

Madge knew Charlene had given him the message. She'd rung Charlene later, just to make sure. That was Fred all over, inconsiderate and selfish. He must realise how much she needed him. And if he wouldn't do it for her, surely he had some feelings for their son. What on earth could be keeping him?

In the darkened motel room, Fred was making love to Susan. He knew it was her first experience, and he took a lot of time over it. He was everything Susan had ever dreamed a lover could be . . . patient, gentle, considerate, sensitive.

She forgot all her guilt, all her misgivings, and gave herself up to the passion of the moment. She had found the most wonderful man in the world — and he was hers.

Chapter 17

MADGE sat numb, as the Judge sentenced Henry to three years jail. Beside her, Charlene started to weep.

She had felt numb ever since the jury had filed back and announced their 'guilty' verdict. There were only a handful of people in the public gallery, and the two men at the press table. Madge recognised one of the reporters, he'd interviewed her once about a social function she'd helped organise. She'd been pleased then at having her name in the papers. Now it was the last thing she wanted — for herself, and for Henry.

The time for waiting for the jury to come out had seemed like forever. Madge could have left the courtroom, but chose to stay there instead. She looked around the place, imprinting it on her mind. It was bare, cheerless, with wood panelled walls and a photo of the Queen hanging over the head of the Judge. In front of the

Judge's chair, a clerk sat writing. Madge made a mental note, without being aware of it, that the place could do with a good re-painting. There was also a cobweb in a corner of the ceiling. Her mind was concentrating on trivialities, trying to keep away from what was going on in the jury room.

When the verdict was announced, Henry had shown no sign of emotion. As he was led from the dock, Madge tried to speak to him. But he turned away from her. She knew he was blaming her for not covering for him. No one had believed Charlene's testimony that he'd been home all evening with her. The prosecutor had been very clever, and had soon had Charlene and Henry's version of a quiet night at home in conflict with each other.

Charlene was nursing her own guilt. She'd wanted to tell the truth about how Henry had helped her that night, but Henry had insisted she keep quiet. He said the court still wouldn't believe her, and it was bad enough for the family that he was in so much trouble. No sense in adding to the problems by telling the world about her pregnancy. Besides, he was positive it wouldn't help. Jacko and Dakka had stuck to their story, insisting Henry had been the mastermind behind the robbery. They'd sworn it was never intended to use violence. Henry had panicked, and lost his head. Their testimony didn't save them, but it got them a lighter sentence. Two years for Jacko, and the same time at a juvenile detention centre for Dakka. And as for Pete, not a word or a trace since that night.

Henry's fate had been sealed from the moment Madge told the cops that he'd said he'd got home just before her. The timing worked in exactly with the warehouse robbery, giving Henry enough time — claimed the police — to do the job, and arrive back just before eleven. The police had testified to what Madge had said. He couldn't give a believable account of how he'd spent the evening. And then there were those fingerprints underneath the dashboard. Henry knew even before the jury foreman announced the verdict. On all three counts — car stealing, robbery and assault — he was found guilty. Guilty of crimes he didn't commit.

Madge, Fred and Charlene arrived home from court. Madge did what she always did when there was a crisis, or she was upset or worried. She put on the kettle to make them all a nice cup of tea.

Charlene said she didn't feel like having anything. She was looking better now than that day when Henry had been arrested, but the past month had been a strain on her. Every day at school, she'd had to endure the whispers and gossip of her school friends. They all knew Henry, and felt sorry for Charlene. But their reaction had been the same as all the others — Henry had done it. Of course, Big Al, Cyn and her close friends had all maintained it wasn't Henry's fault. What could you expect with that gang of no hopers he gets around with ? Blind Freddy could see he was heading for trouble, hanging around with a bunch of creeps like that.

Charlene kept maintaining Henry's innocence, saying he was with her the whole evening. But they all knew how loyal Charlene was to her brother. Loyal enough to lie for him. And then there was the bottle of gin.

Big Al remembered Charlene had said something about going to a party. She'd said it was with Henry's friends, which was unusual for Lennie. Henry's friends weren't the type Lennie hung around with. Big Al remembered commenting on it to her brother at the time.

At recess, the day the news of Henry's arrest broke, she put it to her. "That gin was for Henry, wasn't it?" she asked. "To work up Dutch courage! Getting little sister to run his errands again, or had he run out of money?" The evidence at the court hearing mentioned Jacko and Dakka had been drinking. The cops who'd taken Henry to the station said they'd smelt gin on his clothing — although they'd also had to admit there was no evidence of intoxication. But all in all, things had looked bad.

Charlene went to her room, as Fred and Madge sat down at the kitchen table. Madge reflected that one good thing had come out of all this, Fred had been unusually nice lately. Apart from that day when he hadn't turned up at the station, he had been at pains to get all the legal help he could for Henry. He still blamed Madge for Henry's problems, but at least there hadn't been any violent arguments. Even Charlene had commented on how cheerful her father seemed.

Fred's new attitude had given Madge fresh hope for her marriage. She knew they could never go back to the euphoria of the early days, when love had seemed to make everything so simple. But maybe they could still make something of their relationship. If they both tried, and agreed to forget all their differences. With Henry gone, Madge yearned for affection and companionship. Charlene barely spoke to her, and when she did it was to accuse her of betraying Henry. Madge was feeling increasingly isolated, left on her own. But if she and Fred could pick up the threads of marriage again, try to make a go of it . . .

"Well, got to get going," said Fred, getting to his feet. "I might be working back, don't keep dinner for me tonight.

"Can't you take time off?" asked Madge. "Today of all days. I thought we'd sit down and have a long talk."

"What about?" asked Fred.

Madge hesitated, nervous to broach the subject.

"Our marriage," she said. "We need to discuss it."

Fred's face darkened, but he quickly hid his irritation with a smile.

"Some other time," he said. "Not now, Madge."

Madge still persisted, not wanting to be left on her own. But Fred reminded her they still had legal fees to pay. Trying to get Henry off the hook had cost them plenty. This wasn't the time to neglect the business, they'd need all the money they could make. Besides, there were customers depending on him. And it wasn't fair on Susan to leave her to run both shop and office. She was only a young girl, comparatively inexperienced. She still needed one of them to take charge.

As Fred reached the door, he seemed to soften. Turning back a moment, he kissed Madge goodbye. It wasn't something he normally did, and the gesture gave Madge hope.

"Don't worry, love," he said. "Everything's going to be all right."

Later, to take her mind off things, Madge
opened the morning mail. It had arrived while
they'd been at the court, but she hadn't had the
heart to look at it earlier. A couple of bills. A
note from one of her fellow committee members
commiserating with her on 'that unfortunate
business with Henry'. Madge ripped it up and
threw it in the bin.

There was a letter with an unfamiliar hand-
writing, bearing the postmark Erinsborough.
When Madge opened it, she found it was from
an old friend she hadn't heard from in years.
She'd known them all when they were young,
and had written a few times since then — once
to congratulate Madge on her marriage, and
then for the birth of the children. But that had
been a long time ago. Madge had almost forgotten her.

This time it wasn't for congratulations. It was
to express regret that Max Ramsay's marriage
had broken up. The news of the breakup came
as shock to Madge. But what was an even bigger
shock was that no one had told her about it. It
had come from someone who was now almost a
stranger.

The letter mentioned Max's wife Maria had
gone off to Hong Kong with her lover, and left

179

Max on his own with his two sons. Madge tried to work out how old they'd be now. Shane must be at around twenty-one or twenty-two. And Danny was a bit younger than Henry.

Poor Max. Madge remembered his wedding, and how head over heels in love he'd been with his beautiful young wife. She'd lent Max half the money to buy the house in Ramsay Street, almost on the same spot where the old house stood when they were kids.

Why hadn't anyone told her about Max's marriage problems? Surely her parents knew, even if Max's pride wouldn't allow him to confide in his only sister. Pride was always one of Max's failings, she remembered that. And pig-headed stubbornness. He could never admit to being wrong.

Thinking about Max's marriage problems reminded her suddenly of her own. Maybe it was time her family started to pull together, to help each other through the crisis of Henry going to jail.

She didn't want to finish up like Max, lonely and embittered. Perhaps she had been difficult to get along with at times. Fred's goodbye kiss and warmth this morning seemed to promise hope for the future. What was that he'd said as he was leaving? Everything is going to turn out all right.

Madge made a resolution there and then. There wouldn't be two marriage failures in the Ramsay family. She would put on her best dress, do her hair, and go down to the shop to help Fred finish up. Then they'd go out to dinner, somewhere special, and have a good talk about their marriage. Madge knew she'd nagged too much in the past — she'd tell Fred she was sorry. All she had to do was to make him see she meant what she said about improving their marriage. It was never too late, Madge told herself. There was always tomorrow.

*   *   *

It was past closing time when Madge arrived at the hardware store. True to her promise, she had put on her best dress, and set her hair the way she knew Fred liked it. At the last minute, she had also got out the bottle of French perfume Henry gave her at Christmas, and splashed some behind each ear. She felt as nervous and excited as a young girl on a first date . . . almost like the time Fred had first taken her out, after the dance.

The shop was locked and in darkness, but there was a light out at the back. Madge let herself in with her key, quietly, knowing Fred would be working in the office. She would surprise him, put her arms around him and tell him she still loved him. It would be almost like old times.

As Madge approached the office, she began to hear voices and a woman's laughter. The voices sounded intimate, urgent . . . and she knew instantly what was happening. Madge hesitated, wondering whether to leave quietly or go in. Then she steeled herself to keep walking towards the closed door with the thin streak of light showing under it.

Madge paused a moment outside the door, still hearing the low voices, and then pushed it open. Fred and Susan were in a passionate embrace, with the top buttons of Susan's blouse undone. And from their close familiarity, Madge knew it wasn't the first time. Neither saw her, until it was too late.

Madge felt sick to her stomach. She wanted to say something, but couldn't. Tears stinging her eyes, she turned and walked away.

Chapter 18

MADGE sat in the cab on her way to the airport, thinking back on the last few days.

Fred hadn't come home that night, after she'd walked in on him and Susan in the office. She'd lain awake all night, waiting for him, but he'd stayed away. Next morning he'd come to get some clothes, and tell her he was moving out. She'd told him not to bother, she was the one who would go.

Madge wiped the tears away, as she remembered the last, bitter fight. She had made a scathing attack on Susan, only to have Fred and Charlene both defend her. Fred was bad enough — telling her it was no wonder he turned to someone like Susan, when she was so hard and such a harpy. Susan knew how to behave like a real woman, she was soft and loving and kind. Madge could take that from Fred, it was typical of him. But she was shocked to have Charlene come in on Fred's side. Charlene had said some

183

cruel things, words that Madge would take a long time to forgive or forget.

Madge thought back to the night she'd asked Charlene to come with her. She'd put aside her pride and dignity to plead, telling Charlene it was for her own good.

"Please, Charlene," she'd begged. "You can't stay here, after what your father's done to me."

Charlene had given her a withering look of scorn.

"You should talk," she said. "What you've done to him, you mean. All these years, on his back for every little thing . . . nag, nag, nag. It's a wonder he's put up with it for so long."

Madge's face tightened.

"And what about him and Susan?" she asked.

"I happen to like Susan," retorted Charlene. "She's a nice girl . . . if she makes Dad happy, then good luck to her. At least she'll give him a lot more than he's got from you."

Charlene's words had hurt. Madge hadn't shown it in front of her daughter, but later she'd gone to her room and cried. It was then she decided she would get out of Coffs Harbour. She'd go to the airport first thing in the morning. But there was one more thing to do — try and see Henry.

She'd applied for special permission, telling the prison authorities she was leaving the state.

They'd been sympathetic and compassionate, and had allowed her extra time for the visit. She'd made Henry's favourite cake, and taken it along with her. At the jail, they'd asked her to wait in the reception area, while they went to get Henry. Ten minutes later one of the prison officials came back.

He tried to break the news as kindly as possible, but he said Henry didn't want to see her. He'd tried to persuade him, but Henry had simply refused.

The official could see Madge was upset, and took her off for a cup of tea. He explained first time offenders, especially of Henry's age, could sometimes be difficult. They felt ashamed to face their parents, and so rejected them. You mustn't take it personally, Mrs Mitchell, said the official. Just give the lad a bit of time, and it will all come good.

But Madge knew it wouldn't. She knew now for certain that Henry hadn't forgiven her. And with Charlene on the side of Fred and Susan, Madge felt there was no one left.

Never mind, there were still people who needed her. Max, for one. He hadn't sounded too enthusiastic when she rang and said she was coming down. But Max was like that. Gruff on the outside, marshmallow on the inside. His bark had always been worse than his bite.

But Shane had seemed pleased to hear from her. He was working as a chauffeur now. He said he'd be at the airport to meet her. Madge was looking forward to seeing her nephew.

Madge looked out the window, and remembered the first time she'd come to Coffs Harbour. All those years ago . . . as a young bride, in love, looking forward to a new life. The years of struggle, buying their first home, having babies. So much happiness. And now so much sorrow.

Never mind, thought Madge, as the cab turned a corner and the airport came in sight. Away from the place she'd been betrayed by her husband, she could make a new start.

Some day she'd make a new home for herself, where she'd be loved and wanted. Some day she'd have a place for Henry to come back to, when he got out of prison . . . perhaps even Charlene would lose her bitterness, and give her a second chance.

That's all I want, Madge thought — a second chance at happiness.

Perhaps I'll find it in Ramsay Street.

THE END

186

A Selected List of Fiction Available from Mandarin Books

While every effort is made to keep prices low, it is sometimes necessary to increase prices at short notice. Mandarin Paperbacks reserves the right to show new retail prices on covers which may differ from those previously advertised in the text or elsewhere.

The prices shown below were correct at the time of going to press.

☐	7493 0003 5	**Mirage**	James Follett	£3.99
☐	7493 0005 1	**China Saga**	C. Y. Lee	£3.50
☐	7493 0009 4	**Larksghyil**	Constance Heaven	£2.99
☐	7493 0012 4	**The Falcon of Siam**	Axel Aylwyn	£3.99
☐	7493 0018 3	**Daughter of the Swan**	Joan Juliet Buck	£3.50
☐	7493 0020 5	**Pratt of the Argus**	David Nobbs	£3.50
☐	7493 0025 6	**Here Today**	Zoë Fairbairns	£3.50

TV and Film Titles

☐	7493 0002 7	**The Bill III**	John Burke	£2.99
☐	7493 0055 8	**Neighbours I**	Marshall/Kolle	£2.99
☐	423 02020 X	**Bellman and True**	Desmond Lowden	£2.50
☐	416 13972 8	**Why the Whales Came**	Michael Morpurgo	£2.50
☐	7493 0017 5	**Adventures of Baron Munchausen**	McKeown/Gilliam	£2.99

All these books are available at your bookshop or newsagent, or can be ordered direct from the publisher. Just tick the titles you want and fill in the form below.

Mandarin Paperbacks, Cash Sales Department, PO Box 11, Falmouth, Cornwall TR10 9EN.

Please send cheque or postal order, no currency, for purchase price quoted and allow the following for postage and packing:

UK	55p for the first book, 22p for the second book and 14p for each additional book ordered to a maximum charge of £1.75.
BFPO and Eire	55p for the first book, 22p for the second book and 14p for each of the next seven books, thereafter 8p per book.
Overseas Customers	£1.00 for the first book plus 25p per copy for each additional book.

NAME (Block Letters) ....

ADDRESS ....

....